DREAMING OF HIS CONVENIENT KISS

Cowboy Mountain Christmas

Book 2

JESSIE GUSSMAN

This is a work of fiction. Similarities to real people, places, or events are entirely coincidental. Copyright © 2020 by Jessie Gussman.

Written by Jessie Gussman.

All rights reserved.

No portion of this book may be reproduced in any form without written permission from the publisher or author, except as permitted by U.S. copyright law.

Contents

Acknowledgments

Cover art by Lara Wynter
Editing by Heather Hayden
Narration by Jay Dyess
Author Services by CE Author Assistant

Listen to the unabridged audio for FREE performed by Jay Dyess on the Say with Jay channel on YouTube. Get early access to all of Jay's recordings and listen to Jessie's books before they're available to the general public, plus get daily Bible readings by Jay and bonus scenes by becoming a Say with Jay channel member.

Chapter One

atalie Mooney sat at her kitchen table, her divorce papers in front of her.

The children were in bed, and she didn't swipe at the one lone tear that tracked down her cheek.

This wasn't the way she expected her life to turn out.

When she married Eric, she'd never dreamed she'd eventually be sitting at a rickety, Formica-topped, metal table, in a termite-eaten farmhouse, in the foothills of the Ozark Mountains in Arkansas, staring at the paper that was supposed to dissolve five years of her life.

It contained the ashes of her little-girl dreams.

The memories of late nights alone, wondering where he was.

Early mornings the same, only with their children around.

Hospital stays where she farmed her children out to neighbors between contractions, because her husband had to take a business trip.

When she'd questioned him, he'd gotten angry.

It'd taken her years, but when she cleaned out his car, and found the underwear that wasn't hers, and confronted him with it, and he'd denied it at first, but then he let loose with all the things she lacked and all the reasons he needed to find someone else, she'd made up her mind.

He threatened her with physical harm and shoved her into a wall, using his fist on her cheek.

The next time he came home from a business trip, she wasn't there.

Tapping her finger on the table, she looked at the paper and the little perfect circle of wetness that had fallen off her cheek and slowly seeped onto the bottom of it.

Directly beside that, her phone lay on the table, the screen blank.

She didn't need it to be on to know what would pop up when she pressed the button.

Her house was condemned, and she had two weeks left to move.

This place had been dirt cheap. Still, she'd barely been able to afford it with the telemarketing job she did all afternoon and at night after the children went to bed.

She hadn't found another place to compare with the price.

She wasn't being picky. She'd take anything, anything at all that would keep her children with her. All five of them.

That's what had led her to the site that was on her phone now. Marriageofconvenience.com.

It was supposed to be a Christian site, and everyone was supposed to be vetted. She'd put her application in. It had taken her two weeks to be approved, so she thought they were pretty thorough in their vetting.

It was three o'clock in the morning, and she'd spent the last six hours going through the site.

She'd chosen someone.

There were no names on the site—just nicknames—to preserve privacy. When they were both comfortable with each other, they'd reach out to the admins together, and their names would be released to each other. She liked that added bit of security.

The man she'd chosen had included his email address in his

profile—not all of them had—and she felt like she wanted to reach out that way.

She just wasn't sure what to say.

Maybe she should wait until morning when she was more rested, less emotional.

Seeing the finality of her divorce had been more unsettling than she had thought it would be.

Eric didn't have any claim on her heart. Not anymore, and he hadn't for a long time, but it was more that those papers represented the death of everything she'd hoped her life would be and had put her into the ranks of divorcee, had put her children into the ranks of single-parent home, had given her an "ex," and rang with a finality she hadn't expected.

Her body felt painful and numb at the same time. She hadn't known it could do that.

Picking up her phone, she pulled up the mail app and typed in his email address: wilderman@ourmail.com.

The creaks and groans of the little old house didn't bother her at all, nor did the blowing of the wind or the quietness of the kitchen.

Outside, Natalie had to be brave. She had five children watching her.

Inside, she was scared to death.

Her thumbs hovered above her phone. She tried to figure out how best to word her request.

Dear Mr. Wilder Man,

She looked at that. It seemed a little formal for someone she was planning to offer marriage to.

She deleted the "Mr." then put it back in.

His profile said he was a white-collar worker, married once for five years, divorced, and on good terms with the ex. Two children that his wife had custody of, and he had two days of visitation every two weeks. She deliberately looked for someone with a job that didn't include traveling, and his did not. Although he hadn't gone into detail about what he did, just termed it office worker in finance.

She had no idea what that was. Anything from a bank teller to an accountant, she supposed.

Regardless, it sounded appropriately boring and did not involve travel.

Her standards were not high, but she did have them.

She wasn't doing a repeat of Eric. What was the point of living life and making mistakes if one didn't learn from them?

I saw your profile on marriageofconvenience.com. This email is in regards to that.

You can view my profile HERE, but I wanted to tell you a little bit about myself and make my case.

I'm faithful and loyal. I will be completely devoted to you and you alone. I do not need, do not expect, and do not want to be showered with flowers or candy or gifts or any other silly romantic thing.

I've gotten to the point in my life where none of that matters.

Here, she paused, because she was only 23 years old.

Funny how she felt so much older. So. Much. Older.

She'd gotten pregnant at 15, and instead of learning from that mistake, she had another baby before her classmates graduated from high school.

She hadn't. Graduated, that is. She'd had two children.

Water under the bridge.

She was going to learn from that mistake. And every other mistake she made in her life. She was done being stupid.

Probably shouldn't put that in her letter, although she wanted to. *Dear Wilder Man, I'm done being stupid.*

She wasn't exactly selling herself with that.

As she looked back at her phone, her thumbs started moving again.

Your profile said you wanted a traditional wife, and I can assure you that is definitely what I intend to be. I will cook for you, do your laundry, clean your house, I'll even take care of the yard work and vehicle maintenance. You will be well taken care of.

She read that over. Did she sound too eager? It was all true—she wasn't afraid of working, and she wasn't afraid to serve someone else if he was going to provide for her; after all, she didn't even have a high school diploma, so what other kind of job was she going to get —so she left it.

You also said in your profile that you intended to have a real marriage with the intimacies that that entailed. I'm prepared to do that also.

She paused again. That was the one thing she wasn't sure of. It was part of being married, and other than that, his profile was perfect.

She shoved her doubts aside. As long as he was kind to her children, she'd do anything.

As you can see from my profile, I have five children. The only thing I ask in return is that you're kind to them and provide us with basic necessities. Roof, food, and clothes, and I assure you I'm very frugal.

She hadn't had a choice. Getting pregnant at fifteen, when she was too young to hold down any type of full-time job, had definitely taught her to be frugal.

Maybe she should have made some different choices, but it was too late now. Better to not think about them.

She chewed on a fingernail before she added:

I do have a bit of a time constraint. I need to make a decision in two weeks.

She hadn't wanted to come across as desperate, but she felt like she needed to add that last bit, so he knew he couldn't mess around with his response.

> *I would appreciate an immediate reply, if possible, because of that time issue. I will not contact anyone else for twenty-four hours while I wait to hear from you.*
>
> *Sincerely,*
>
> *Mom of Five*

Chapter Two

*D*enver Barclay sat on the upper deck of the ship that carried the underwater welding crew and supplies in the Gulf of Mexico and stared at his phone.

He'd never gotten a stranger email.

Honestly, he couldn't decide whether it was a prank or whether the woman was serious and actually thought he had a profile on some "marriage of convenience" site.

He'd already checked it out. The site existed, although whether or not it was legit was a good question.

He definitely didn't have a profile on it, though.

Not that he didn't want to be married, just...

He looked out over the open sea, blue stretching out as far as he could see. Blue on the horizon, a slightly different shade, and that blue stretched overhead from one end of his vision to the other.

The sea was calm, flat as glass.

Staring at it too long would make his eyes cross, if not close. He'd just put in an eighty-hour work week, and he was exhausted.

But that's the way it was for an underwater welder. Feast or famine. Right now was feast, and he pushed his body, as he had for the last fifteen years, to do what needed to be done.

He'd passed the three-decade mark and was looking pretty hard at thirty-five. He could feel the years catching up with him.

But he didn't want stop, didn't want to slow down, could hardly stand the slow winter months of December, January, and February when things screeched to a crawl and he had nothing to do but to think about the emptiness, the void, the black hole.

He'd actually taken to volunteering as an EMT when he wasn't hanging out in South America. He needed the rush, the activity, the action. The adrenaline high. Whatever it was, he wasn't any good at slowing down or stopping.

Maybe he needed to learn. Because he'd just bought a farm. If that wasn't slowing down, he didn't know what was.

After fifteen years as an underwater welder, he didn't need to farm to make money. He just bought it because...

Dark curly hair and laughing blue eyes materialized in his mind, clear and perfect and beautiful.

She needed a man like his brother Ethan, someone dependable, salt of the earth, without the need to fill the emptiness in his soul with danger and adrenaline.

She had children to think about.

He looked at his phone again. This woman had children to think about too.

One of the deckhands shouted, and one of his weld crew shouted back, and Denver lifted his eyes, making sure everything was okay. In addition to being a certified diver and a certified welder, he had his medical technician certification as well. Any accidents on board, and they would be coming to him.

Which was exactly what he wanted. He didn't want to stand on the sidelines, staring hopelessly. He wanted to be in the action, doing something.

His hand tightened on his phone.

He'd wondered about his purpose in life. What could he do? What had he done? What was he here for?

This woman had kids that needed taking care of; she needed a man to provide for her.

He almost snorted at her line that she was willing to do "that."

She sounded prim.

But he liked loyalty and valued it. Faithfulness.

A sense of humor was always nice. But he wasn't sure he was planning on spending any more time at home than he did now, so it might not matter.

She needed someone to support her and help her take care of her children, because obviously, it was difficult for a single mom with young children to work outside the home.

He could provide what she needed, what she was asking for.

They didn't even have to get married.

She could live in the farmhouse he'd just bought.

"Denver. Get down here. We need you. Suit up."

Denver scrambled up, shoving his phone in his pocket. He was exhausted, having gotten less than four hours of sleep each night this week, but this was exactly what he wanted. Motion and busyness.

He jogged over to the ladder. He'd answer that letter later when he wasn't so tired and was able to think clearly.

Normal people did not offer strangers marriages of convenience. The woman had to be a quack.

WELL, the man had taken all of the allotted twenty-four hours to think about it.

Twenty-three hours and forty-five minutes had gone by, and Natalie again sat at her kitchen table, only this time in the dark, because she didn't need to look at her divorce papers.

Honestly, she'd given up hope that the man she'd emailed was going to respond. She was just waiting for the time to expire so she could write to the next guy she'd chosen.

Unsurprisingly, she hadn't gotten a single response from her profile on marriageofconvenience.com.

It was probably the five kids. That seemed to do it.

Although maybe it was her picture. She was twenty-three, but she looked like she was about forty in the picture. She felt like forty, too.

Maybe she should just say she was forty, and then people wouldn't think she was lying.

A sound from her computer startled her, and she sat up straight.

A new message.

Welder Man came up in her inbox.

Her brows furrowed.

Wasn't it *Wilder* Man?

That's what she'd been thinking. That's what she thought she'd typed in.

Before she opened the email, she went into her sent items and pulled up the message she'd sent yesterday.

She put a hand on her head with a slap and laughed, not liking the way it sounded—kind of wild and a little bit like she'd been living in the woods for three years by herself with long scraggly hair and a dress made out of grape leaves.

She could deny it all she wanted to, but that was exactly how her laugh sounded.

She was such an idiot.

She pressed the button for inbox again and scrolled over, checking the box and going to the garbage can. The cursor hovered over the garbage can icon while she thought about it.

It was embarrassing enough to make this mistake. She didn't really want to read about the guy laughing hysterically at her. Or worse yet, asking why anyone in their right mind would be offering a marriage of convenience to a complete stranger.

Or even worse than that, maybe she accidentally sent it to a policeman or government official, who thought she was doing some kind of scam thing.

She hadn't even realized that marriageofconvenience.com existed until recently. She wasn't completely sure it was legal. She hadn't even thought to look it up.

That'd be just great. How could she take care of her children from jail?

Did she want to know if the police were coming to arrest her?

She hit the garbage can icon, and the email disappeared.

Closing her computer, she took it to the counter where she plugged it in.

How much time did one get sentenced in jail for propositioning a police officer?

Or government official.

Maybe it was a federal offense. She didn't want to go to prison.

Dragging a hand along the table, feeling for her phone, she grabbed it and started out of the kitchen.

Maybe she should Google it. At least she'd know how much time she was looking at. She couldn't afford a lawyer. Plus, she was guilty. It was there in writing. She just propositioned someone. Maybe they'd get her on child endangerment.

What was she thinking?

She hadn't been, obviously. Like the rest of her life.

No one was ever gonna believe that she was actually doing this to try to keep her children safe, not to expose them to more danger.

Yeah, that would go over well.

No one was going to believe her. No one ever did.

But she wasn't going to be a victim.

She stopped short. She wasn't going to run from her problems either.

She wasn't going to run from this.

She would face it, head-on.

You ran from Eric.

That was different. She hadn't had a choice. She'd do whatever it took to keep her kids safe. In that instance, it meant leaving.

Lifting her phone up, she clicked and swiped until her deleted emails came up. Clicking on the one she'd just trashed, she waited while it loaded.

Her chest had that slightly hurt feel, like all the air in it was laced with shards of glass. Her hand shook, but only a little. She would deal with whatever she had to deal with.

The email wasn't very long, and she slowly leaned against the doorjamb as she read down through it.

Dear Mom of Five,

I'm not the person you meant to send the email to. I don't have any profiles on any marriage of convenience sites. I didn't know there were marriage of convenience sites.

Be careful, it might not be legit.

Sounds like you're in a tough spot. Sorry I can't help. I'm not stateside and won't be until just before the holidays.

If I can help out then, let me know.

Sincerely,

Welder Man

By the time she was done reading, Natalie had sunk down the doorframe but wasn't as embarrassed as she'd thought she might be.

She hadn't expected to get a yes with her first inquiry, and certainly not from someone who wasn't even supposed to have read her letter.

He hadn't said anything about the kids, but if he wasn't even in the states, it wouldn't have influenced his opinion.

At least he returned her email. She should write and thank him. It did sound like he might help her if she needed it when he was back, although it could just be lip service, too.

She sighed, pulling her legs up and putting her forehead on her knees. Life was so hard. She didn't want to do this. Didn't want to proposition men she didn't even know. But what else could she do?

It was too late to go back and fix the mistakes she'd made at fifteen and nineteen and all the stupid stuff in between. She had to somehow live with what she'd done, but how?

Could she keep her family together?

Maybe her kids would be better off with someone else.

No!

She'd learned from her mistakes. She'd fixed the problems she had. Her kids could see her working hard and see her getting up after she'd fallen and trying again.

Lord?

She didn't expect God to answer her. It seemed like she screwed her life up enough that God had probably washed His hands of her and gone on to somebody else. She really didn't have anything to offer Him anyway. It was all she could do to stay afloat. It wasn't like she could give money or do something wonderful for the church. If she could get through every day and keep her kids alive, she felt like that was a win.

She didn't have time to do anything for God.

She could only assume He wouldn't have time for her.

As she thought about the Lord, she considered the marriage of convenience site and decided that her first hunch was right—it was a terrible idea. Welder Man was right. It could be a scam or worse.

She'd thought she was that desperate, but she wasn't.

That decision brought peace to the craziness that had been brewing in her heart.

She'd come to Mistletoe not quite a year previous, and in that time, Journee Barclay had become her best friend, even though they really didn't have anything in common.

Journee was a nurse, while Natalie was a high school dropout, but Journee had been sweet and seemed to accept her as she was. She'd been kind to her children as well. They somehow clicked and had fun together.

Pulling her phone out, Natalie pulled up the texting app and typed a message to Journee, knowing that it was possible she might be up in the middle of the night working the late shift.

Are you up?

She hit send. She knew she wouldn't be bothering her if she were sleeping. They'd often texted in the middle of the night when Kole was younger and Natalie was up with him. Journee had told her to text her any time, and of course, Natalie had returned the offer.

Journee had gone through a bad breakup, and Natalie had been there for her.

Sure am, and I'm on break. What's up?

Natalie smiled. Journee's bubbly personality came out in it.

I just need someone to tell me again why I'm supposed to believe and have faith.

They'd had plenty of discussions about it as Journee went through her breakup and struggled to believe that the things she couldn't control were under God's control.

They'd talked about it, and on paper and in conversation, it sounded easy. But actually walking away from the marriage of convenience site, which looked like her only solution, and allowing God to work in her life, and trusting Him was a little harder in reality.

Her phone rang. She should have known Journee wouldn't have the patience to text. She seldom did, unless she was working and grabbing a text between checking patients.

"Hello?" Natalie said, still sitting on the floor, leaning against the doorjamb.

"What's up?"

She didn't want her friend to try to fix her problem; she just wanted a little good advice to get through said problem.

Although Journee already knew she had to move. She just didn't know the extent to which Natalie was financially strapped. Her own fault, of course.

"Remember when we were talking about God being in control? That he allows things to happen?"

There was silence on the phone for a bit, and Natalie could almost see her friend thinking. "I do. I remember we talked a lot about why a good God would allow bad things to happen. And why he wasn't answering my prayer when I begged him to change my situation and fix things between Alex and me, and he just didn't. And yeah, I remember you and I had a lot of conversations about struggling to accept the Lord's will. What's going on?"

Natalie sighed. "I just needed the reminder. I want to do things on my own and take things into my own hands. But we talked about sometimes things being for our good or something."

"That God allows trials in your life to help you grow?"

"Yeah. That, I guess."

"We said if you fail your trial, God gives it to you again and again until you walk through it the way you're supposed to without trying to fix it yourself."

"Yeah. And then how much is too much?"

"What do you mean?"

She meant was it okay to instigate a marriage of convenience from a website she'd found? Ha. She could hardly ask that. Not even of Journee.

"How much of me doing stuff is too much? We're supposed to let God work, but it's not like he does everything while we do nothing. And how am I supposed to know how much I'm supposed to do and when I'm supposed to trust him?"

"I don't know."

Chapter Three

Natalie and Journee sat in silence for a bit.

Maybe there was something comforting in the fact that she was asking a question of her friend, whose dad was a pastor, and she still didn't know the answer.

Was that a sad state of affairs, when she was comforted over a problem that confused her, because it confused someone else too?

She didn't really want to tell her friend that she didn't think God was going to do anything for her anyway. That she was having trouble trusting the Lord to begin with. That she thought that she really didn't deserve His help, and that all made it even worse.

"I think," Journee said slowly, "I think God wants us to do everything we can, within reason, and then trust him to work things out. But I don't think he wants us to panic and start doing a bunch of things that don't make any sense. You know?"

Natalie laughed. "Like we talked about stalking Alex?"

Journee laughed with her. Should she have said anything? It had been a while ago, and Journee seemed to be completely over him, but she'd been so heartbroken at the time and even worse because Alex hadn't really wanted to break up with her, but his parents had pressured him into it, and he'd chosen to make them happy. Which both Journee and Natalie generally admired, because they respected a man who honored his parents, even when he didn't have to.

Unfortunately, that meant Alex walking away from Journee.

"That's exactly right. I *wanted* to do that, and I thought it might help, because he'd see how serious I was about him. But I knew it wasn't the right thing to do. Like, there's no Bible verse that says I can't do that, but it's just not right." She ended that last sentence on a bit of a question, almost as though she couldn't find the words to explain.

"I see. I get it. I'm not sure exactly how you know that's not right. You just know you don't chase after him."

"Maybe, because if *my* parents had been the ones pressuring me to break up with him, and I had decided to honor my parents and leave my boyfriend, I wouldn't have wanted him to chase after me, making me feel guilty for making the decision that I thought was best."

"It's the 'do unto others as you would have them do unto you' thing?"

"Yeah. I guess."

That didn't really apply to the marriage of convenience. Except… maybe she could apply a different concept. The idea that when she was offering someone a marriage of convenience, she of course knew he had been vetted by the website, but she didn't know what his spiritual condition was. And she was offering to yoke herself to someone who might not care about doing right.

"What's the verse about the equal yoking?"

Journee was quiet for a minute, like she was thinking. "'And be not unequally yoked with unbelievers.'"

"Yeah, that one. Thank you."

Funny, because she couldn't think of anything else that would make it wrong. But it still just didn't seem right.

She supposed that probably meant she was better to be safe than sorry and to not do it.

"You know, I'm still not sure why God wouldn't let Alex and me be together. It just doesn't make sense to me. But I've gotten a lot better at realizing his plan is perfect even though sometimes I can't see it."

"I know it is. But, goodness, I *never* can see it."

Journee laughed. "I can't very often either. But you know, there's something so relaxing about taking your mind off your problem and giving it to the Lord. It's hard to do. But when you're able to get it done, yeah."

"I believe you. I'm still working on that getting it done part."

There was a bunch of beeping and a yell in the background, and Journee said, "Hey, I have to go."

"Okay. Thanks."

They hung up, with Natalie feeling a little better but still not quite sure how far exactly she should trust the Lord.

What if he didn't give her a house to live in? What if it was the day she was to be evicted and she was just sitting there, twiddling her thumbs, going "God's gonna save me." She would look stupid. And she'd be letting her children down, because they would have no place to stay.

It was late, and she was going to be tired and probably have a headache in the morning, but she knew if she went upstairs to lie down, she would never go to sleep. Her mind was working overtime but not solving anything.

Maybe, just for the peace of mind, she should try to do what Journee said, but again she felt like she hadn't done enough for God for Him to want to help her. It all came back to that.

Here's your chance to do something for the Lord.

Really? What?

Trust Him.

That's it? How was that doing anything?

But her gram had taken her to Sunday School when she was a kid, and it was surprising how much she'd remembered from those years. Those teachings had been strengthened by the teaching of Pastor Race for the last eight months.

Somehow, it pleased God when she trusted Him.

But, God, I need an answer now! I can't wait.

Wait patiently on the Lord.

She wasn't too big on making deals with the Lord, but she talked to him for just a minute, whispering, because although she was pretty sure her children were sound asleep, she didn't want them to come downstairs and think she was crazy.

Even if she was.

"I can't just sit around and not do anything. I'm not even sure that's what you want me to do anyway. Why else did you give me legs and a mouth, if you were going to do everything for me? But I promise I will try not to worry about it, and I will try even harder not to do anything stupid, like find another marriage of convenience website."

There. It probably wasn't the best offer the Lord had all day, but it was the best she could do.

She started to get up, already feeling better.

Then she froze, remembering something else.

"Oh, Lord? I'll try to trust you, but I'd really prefer my family stay together. It's all I have."

Taking a deep breath, she held it for a few seconds then took a half a minute to blow it out. Her anxiety faded with the breath leaving her body.

She should write Welder Man back. Apologize for being a crazy person and thank him, too. He could have been a jerk or taken advantage of her. Instead, he'd been decent.

She wasn't going to send any more emails out to potential matches, though. She knew that much. The marriage of convenience website was a really bad idea. She couldn't put her finger on exactly what was wrong with it, but she knew her solution didn't lie there.

Bringing her phone up, she pulled up the email app.

It didn't take long to reply and send a few sentences back, and it made her feel better.

Now, how was the Lord going to solve her problem? And what, exactly, did He expect her to do to help him?

The question was still bothering her when she went to church the next morning.

There had to be a solution. A cheap rental that she could afford with her telemarketing job and the little extra money she'd made by working at her neighbor's camp earlier in the summer.

Speaking of whom, the first couple she saw as she parked her car in the church lot and got out was Ethan and Ruby Shuff who had come back from their elopement and honeymoon.

She had to smile. It had been so obvious at camp a few weeks ago that they were totally meant for each other. And Mistletoe was exceptionally lucky and blessed to have a surgeon of Ruby's caliber at their hospital.

Ruby had been trained for bigger and better things than their small town, but Natalie supposed love did that to a person.

Not that she would ever find it out.

The couple walked in, holding hands and whispering to each other.

So sweet.

But it intensified the hurting emptiness in her own chest, the mistakes of her past, and the bleakness of her future.

Maybe, if things hadn't worked out between Ruby and Ethan, she would be asking Ethan right now if she could move into his house.

But even though she was desperate, she wouldn't move herself and her five kids into a newlyweds' home, not when Ethan and Ruby had waited so long and been apart for so much of their lives. This was a special time for them, and she would not, under any circumstances, infringe upon that.

She sighed, opening the back door and unbuckling her baby from his car seat. Having just turned one, Kole wasn't a baby anymore, but since he was the youngest, he'd probably be stuck with that moniker for the rest of his life.

She smiled at his gap-toothed grin and hefted him out of the car seat. Grabbing the baby bag, she made sure her youngest daughters —Sky and Ramona, two and four—were able to get out themselves.

Jack and Maggie, her oldest two children at eight and seven, put the middle seat down and crawled out of the back eagerly.

With summer vacation going on and camp over, church was the only time they saw their friends.

Jack took Sky's hand and Maggie took Ramona's, and they walked across the parking lot to the church. It didn't take any time at all to get the kids settled in their classes and Sky and Kole settled in the nursery.

She went upstairs.

At the top of the steps, she greeted several people as she walked to her normal spot in the pews. She'd not quite reached it when Mrs. Mason, an older lady in the church, came bustling over.

"I heard you might be looking for a house?" Mrs. Mason said, stepping in front of her and breathing kind of heavily from her rushed walk over.

Natalie nodded, her heart kicking up with hope that she hardly dared to allow blossom in her chest. Could Mrs. Mason be her savior? Did she have the answers to her problem?

"I am," she said, clasping her hands together in front of her to keep from grabbing a hold of the lady's arms and falling to her knees begging her to give her something, anything, that signified hope.

"I thought I heard that. I'll put you on our prayer list," Mrs. Mason said, pulling up the pad of paper in her hand and flipping back four or five full pages before she came to the end of the list and jotted Natalie's name down.

There were some really great prayer warriors in the church, and she appreciated it. But looking at that notebook full of names, she'd be asleep before she prayed through the first page. She didn't have a whole lot of confidence in too many people making it the whole way through and getting to the end where her name was.

She supposed the Lord didn't need to have a whole army of people praying for her, but she needed all the help she could get.

"Thank you, Mrs. Mason. I appreciate it." Her words lacked any enthusiasm, and they sounded just as deflated as she felt, probably.

She stood there for a bit as Mrs. Mason bustled away.

She wanted to have faith; truly, she did. But it was so hard.

Not hard to believe that God came through for people, because she'd seen it happen. She knew it did. But not really for people like her.

God came through for great missionaries of faith, preachers and their families, good Christians who'd never screwed up anything.

She'd gotten pregnant at fifteen, and her life had just been one big downward spiral, culminating in an abusive husband whom she left.

Always fiercely independent, she hadn't wanted to have to go to a women's shelter. Not that there was anything wrong with those. She'd go if she had to.

But one of her best friends in high school had told her stories about the shelter that she'd been raised in. The abuse that had gone on, the drug addictions, and the stories of desperate, drug-addicted mothers allowing their boyfriends pay-for-play privileges with their daughters.

The shelter her friend had spent time in was extremely corrupt but probably an anomaly. Probably.

Natalie hadn't wanted to take the chance, hadn't wanted to worry about her children, and hadn't wanted to constantly be watching the people around her. Not that she could do it on her own.

But so far, she had. She'd left her husband, rented a house, and managed to keep her kids together.

This little problem of not being able to find a place to stay would resolve itself, and she would make it.

Her eyes landed on her friend Journee, coming up the side of the church.

Journee smiled and returned Natalie's wave, sliding into the seat they usually shared. Natalie moved to join her.

"How you doing, Natalie?" Joel Kershaw asked from behind her.

Joel was single but at least ten years older than she, and she just couldn't picture him as anything other than a brother.

She took a deep breath, shoving all of her thoughts aside about God and how she wasn't really good enough for Him to answer her prayer and how she didn't deserve to be gotten out of the fix she was in because it was her own fault she was in it to begin with.

Kinda rude to get herself into a fix and then beg God to get her out.

She put a smile on her face that she hoped looked at least half real and tried not to look like she was despondent and depressed.

"It's been an interesting summer," she said, knowing that was at least honest. "How are you?" She wanted to get past the small talk and go sit down. Maybe there would be something in the sermon today that would ease her heart and give her hope.

"I'm doing good." He shifted a little, then rubbed the back of his neck. If she weren't so sure that Joel was completely confident, she would almost say he was nervous. She tried not to tap her foot while she waited for him to spit out whatever it was he wanted to say so she could leave.

"Um," he said, his eyes landing on her shoulder before bouncing over to the window. He stared at it, like he could actually see out of it, or maybe he was just looking at the stained glass. It hadn't changed, she was certain, since last Sunday, but Joel was looking at it like it had, and it was almost enough to make her want to turn her head and try to see what the difference was.

He looked both ways before he lowered his voice. "Are you looking for a house to rent?"

"I am." Again, she tried to keep herself from wilting. She didn't want everybody pitying her. She was at the point where, for her children's sake, she'd accept help, but she didn't want to be the object of everyone's sad glances and charity.

Joel's square jaw bunched, and he ran his hand over his short hair. He was a good-looking man, she supposed. But she was far more interested in the question he just asked about the house. Did he have one?

"I'm supposed to be taking care of my buddy's farm for the next two or three months while he's on assignment. It's a little run-down, but you could live in it until he gets back to the states."

Her mouth dropped. Her heart thundered. A wall of excitement built up and burst inside of her. It was all she could do to keep from skipping around the church screaming "*Yes!*" at the top of her lungs. That would hardly do for a mom of five, even if she was only twenty-three. She felt like she was forty anyway. She lived enough life to have the wisdom of a forty-year-old.

"Are you sure your buddy won't mind?"

"He told me to take care of it as I saw fit. If you need a spot to live, it's yours."

"I'll take it."

"Don't you want to look at it?"

"No. Where I'm living isn't exactly the Hilton. It can't be any worse than that. As long as the roof doesn't leak, and even if it does, I'll take it."

"The roof doesn't leak."

"Sounds good."

He nodded. "You can move in anytime. My buddy was just up and signed the papers and did the title work and the deed transfer. Since he's going to be out of the country, there's no rush, and you can hang out there until you find somewhere else."

"Sounds good. I can start moving stuff this afternoon." She hoped she wasn't being too forward. But why wait?

"If you're gonna do that, I can help you." He moved, almost as though he was ready to walk away, but then he stopped and scratched his head. "Don't know where you live."

"If you know where Ethan Shuff's farm is, I'm on the farm next to his, and you pass the house I'm renting as you're going into his place."

"You're kidding? That house is on the farm my buddy bought." His brows furrowed. "Because of him being gone so much, he trusted me to handle everything… I think he thought that rental was empty."

"It's supposed to be." She didn't want to get into the details of the termites and her landlord telling her she needed to leave.

"We might even be able to get most of your stuff moved this afternoon. I'll see if I can scare up a few helpers, and we'll get this done."

"Sounds good. Thank you."

Natalie went to her seat with a much lighter heart than what she'd entered the church with. Maybe her position at the bottom of the fifth page of Mrs. Mason's prayer list wasn't a bad place to be after all.

Chapter Four

$\mathcal{D}$enver held an orange in one hand and his phone in the other, reading the email that had just come in from Mom of Five.

The sea was slightly less calm but still just as endless, boring to some people maybe, but he loved it.

Although, nothing could take the place of the beautiful Ozark Mountains where he'd grown up.

The sea would probably always have a piece of his heart, but without even really thinking about it, he supposed he'd always figured that he'd end up back in the Ozarks and spend the rest of his life there, once he'd outlived the shelf life of an underwater welder.

A decade ago, that shelf life had seemed pretty long.

Today, after the week he'd had, it felt short and almost over.

One of his buddies lay in the sick bay, burns on his arm and neck.

Denver had seen worse, and the guy would recover. Almost certainly recover. They weren't headed home, and they were too far out for him to be lifted off in a chopper. Their job wasn't scheduled to end until October.

He chuckled to himself a little, because for the first time in his life, he almost wished he were headed home sooner.

Mom of Five had sent him another email, and he found himself reading it over and wanting more than anything to write something back.

He started at the beginning of her email and read it through again.

Dear Welder Man,

I wanted to thank you so much for your kind reply. Obviously, my email went to the wrong person, and I appreciate you replying and letting me know.

I also appreciate the little bit of advice that you gave. Maybe that's what I needed to hear, since it got me thinking, and ultimately, I decided that you are right; it wasn't worth the risk to use the marriage of convenience site.

You didn't have to take the time to send an email or give me the advice, and I appreciate both.

Wherever you are—I'm picturing you in California, maybe in Napa Valley, taking care of your almond trees—I hope you're safe and happy and blessed.

Tell me what brand you are, and I'll buy a bag of nuts the next time I'm in the store.

Sincerely,

Mom of Five

It made him laugh every time. So whimsical.

Where did she even get that? Napa Valley? Almond trees?

He looked around, ocean stretching out in every direction, underneath and all around the big hulking shape of the ship that he was on, in the middle of the Atlantic Ocean, miles from civilization, and months before he'd be anywhere near a tree of any kind, let alone an almond tree, and yet the idea kind of made him laugh, had definitely given him a smile.

He hadn't answered right away and had worked another eighty-hour week, but any time he'd had a break of just a few minutes, he'd brought her email up and had another laugh.

He'd gone back and forth all week, but he'd finally decided…he was going to answer her.

"Taps" began to play. Brennon, who had played the trumpet in the military was part of his crew and it was just something the guy did every evening he wasn't working.

The sun sank slowly over the horizon. It was the most beautiful time of day. No matter how many times Denver heard "Taps," it still stirred his soul, and there was nothing better than watching the sun go down as he listened.

As the last notes faded away, he looked again at his phone. There was something really appealing about a woman with a sense of humor.

Maybe it was his working environment, where he lived the danger every day. For years, he'd done the dangerous thing. Something about electricity and water that didn't mix and then he added the flammable explosive gases in on top of it, and he had a recipe for disaster if he weren't paying attention.

Then of course he had the deep diving on top of it, the danger of sharks, the bends, the unexpected currents, and the guy next to him making a mistake. There was an almost certain expectation that something was going to go wrong. Sometime.

Still, he felt good because he was doing something worthwhile.

He looked at his phone again.

He and this woman couldn't be any more different. She with her five kids looking for a husband, and he on a boat in the middle of nowhere doing a job that was too dangerous for most people to even think about. Single. Alone. On a ship with only men.

He had three sisters that he loved with all his heart…he also knew another woman. One who had small children—he didn't even know how many—who had recently married his brother.

Apparently, they'd eloped. He didn't really have any details. All his dad said the last time they talked was that his brother Ethan had gotten married and was on his honeymoon.

Since there was no wedding planned, he assumed it was an

elopement. And since, as far as he knew, Ethan hadn't had a girlfriend, his neighbor was the only one he could think of who Ethan would have married.

Denver wished now, for maybe the first time, that his job had given him a little more time to stay stateside. He would have liked to have helped his brother with the camp and gotten to know that woman a little better.

She'd intrigued him.

But, on second thought, no. It was better that it happened the way it did. He wouldn't have wanted to have fallen in love with the woman his brother married.

No, God had definitely saved him from that mistake. Although, when he closed his eyes, she was the woman who came to mind.

He was gonna have to change that. Picking up his phone, he pulled up his email app and began to write.

Dear Mom of Five,

You don't have to thank me. I didn't do anything for you that I wouldn't have done for one of my sisters. I have a bunch of those.

Your email made me laugh, and I couldn't resist writing back, although I don't know why. I guess we don't have anything more to say to each other.

Maybe I want to thank you for the smile.

My job, which I love, is difficult and dangerous. In the past three weeks, I put in more than eighty hours each week. Your email was the bright spot in this past week. Although, I had to be careful not to smile around the other guys, because then they'd ask me what I thought was so funny. I could hardly admit I didn't even know the name of the person who sent me the email that made me smile.

So, no. I'm not in the Napa Valley, and I don't own a single almond tree. But I like the whimsical idea. Sometimes real life can be brutal. I've got a buddy in the sick bay right now, with burns over both arms and his face. He's gonna live, but he's in a lot of pain. It was an accident that could have been avoided.

I'm not much for avoiding real life or living in a fantasy world, but rather than the

Napa Valley and almond trees, I think I'd like to be in the Ozarks, or maybe the foothills, and grow some corn and maybe raise some cows. Not as romantic, but it's a nice daydream nonetheless.

I suppose, since you did the honors first, it's my turn to make a guess about you. I bet you're a city girl.

I want to say New York City, but everybody says that, so how about Baltimore? That's a nice city along the bay. You're there, in a big high-rise apartment, with glass walls overlooking the bay and the sunrise in your living room, but you're not in your living room, because you're lounging in a chair beside the pool watching your children swim.

How'd I do?

Take care. I'm glad you gave up the marriage of convenience site.

Sincerely,

Welder Man

"MOM, are you going to finish reading the story?"

"Mom? Put your phone down, Mom. You said you'd read us the story. You're not done."

Natalie shook her head, coming out of her trance to hear her children fussing. And rightfully so. She thought she probably stopped in midsentence as soon as her phone had dinged with the notification that there had been an email.

When "Welder Man" had come up on her screen, she hadn't bothered to look back at the book.

That said something about her sad existence, didn't it? When she got excited over the email of a person she didn't even know.

"I'm sorry, children, I got sidetracked." She put her phone down and picked the book up, looking over the top of it at Ramona, whose eyes and nose were sticking out of the covers, but her mouth was covered and her little hands clutched her blankets with white knuckles. "Don't demand that your mother has to do anything. You can ask kindly, saying 'please,' but I don't want to hear that tone out of you again."

Ramona's brows trembled, and her eyes went down. "Yes, ma'am," she whispered.

"And I'm sorry. You're right, I shouldn't have stopped in the middle of a sentence to look at my email. I'll try to do better."

She picked up her book and started reading again, but her mind wasn't really on the story. She'd read it a million times, though, so she was still able to do the voices and put expression into it and make the kids laugh, but she'd been thinking about Welder Man.

Should she answer him?

She kinda figured she had thanked him and that would be the end of it.

She added that last bit about the almond trees just to be goofy, because even though she was a serious and wise Mom of Five, she was still a kid at heart, and she hadn't been able to keep her silly side contained.

Maybe, because she thought she'd never hear from him again, she'd felt a little more free to say something completely off the wall.

He hadn't said exactly where he was, but he worked a hard job having those kinds of hours. Then he said he couldn't say anything to the other guys, so obviously he was around just men.

She laughed. Maybe he was in prison.

Were prisoners allowed to send emails? Maybe that's why it had taken so long for him to respond. Maybe they could only send emails on certain days.

That would be a mistake she hadn't made yet.

"Why are you laughing, Mom?" Maggie asked.

"Sorry. That wasn't a funny part, was it?" Man, kids noticed everything.

At least they'd managed to move into their new house.

Funny, that Welder Man would want to be in the Ozarks where she was. She didn't know him, though, and thought it might be best not to admit that to him. Still...

Maybe she would email Welder Man back. Because yeah, he was pretty far off the mark too.

❄

Dear Welder Man,

Originally, I emailed you because I was in a pretty desperate situation. But after being convicted about running ahead of the Lord, along with your statement about that website, and some advice from a good friend, I changed my course.

So funny how that works, because the very next day God provided a house for me. It's not a permanent thing, but the lion is not at the door anymore, at least.

I guess you missed the mark too, because I'm not anywhere near Baltimore, and I'm not in an apartment either, and my kids have never swum in a swimming pool.

However, rather than almond trees, we have fruit trees!

I've kind of lucked into this, because the previous owner had been taking care of them, and they are ready to harvest now.

I didn't realize this, because I wasn't here this time last year, but I guess life is full of new experiences?

I have to admit I like the idea of glass walls. I like to look out when I can't be out.

Eighty hours sounds like a long week, and your job doesn't sound like fun.

Sincerely,

Mom of Five

Dear Mom of Five,

I like the idea that we don't know each other's names.

Sometimes I feel like I'm playing in a very bad B movie.

Been thinking lately about God's plan versus what I want. When I was younger, I didn't really consider God's plan.

But I can't remember a time when I didn't want to be an underwater welder. I don't even know where I heard of it for the first time.

We get older, and our perspective shifts.

Be happy,

Welder Man

PS I like hot sauce.

Chapter Five

Dear Welder Man,

If your life is a B movie, mine has to be at least a C-. Do they grade us?

It's funny that you mentioned God's plan. I've been thinking along the same lines. I messed up when I was younger. Can I expect God to give me help?

I've always been a big believer in taking personal responsibility for what you've done and not taking the easy way out. But how much of that is me working, and how much of that is me sitting back and letting God do it?

I haven't figured out the answer.

See straight,

Mom of Five

PS I'm short.

Dear Mom of Five,

I have no idea about the movies. I don't watch many, although there's not too much else to do in your downtime on the ship. It's not exactly a cruise ship.

I'd rather be working if I'm awake. And usually am.

God will help you. He says so. He doesn't say that you have to have certain prequalifications. Does he?

I think the hard part is letting go of what you want. Because most of the time, what we want isn't what God wants for us. We fight for what we want, or we spend a lot of time trying to rationalize why what we want is what God wants. At least that's what I do.

Be good,

Welder Man

PS Cardinals all the way.

Dear Welder Man,

I guess He doesn't say that He requires prequalifications, but I feel like He should. And I don't qualify. So that makes me feel like I need to do it on my own. Which is definitely not something you find in Scripture. So that leaves me floundering.

See the light,

Mom of Five

PS I hate baseball.

Dear Mom of Five,

I'm thinking you can't go by your feelings. In fact, I'm pretty sure you shouldn't.

I think it's probably a matter of letting go of the worry and working as hard as you can while admitting that God is in control.

Just my thought, though, because I don't have it figured out.

Be better,

Welder Man

PS I'm not sure we can still be friends.

Dear Welder Man,

Really? We can't be friends because I don't like baseball? Isn't that shallow?

See beyond yourself,

Mom of Five

PS I'm afraid to admit anything else.

Dear Mom of Five,

You talked me into making an exception. Don't tell anyone.

Be you,

Welder Man

PS I guess I can't if you can't.

Dear Welder Man,

I'm the only person you're friends with who doesn't like baseball? I'm sorry, but you need to get out more.

I'm putting the kids to bed. Then I'm going to pray for my direction and for you to break out of your bubble.

See the world,

Mom of Five

PS Peanut butter or jelly?

Dear Mom of Five,

I'll work on getting out more.

There was supposed to be a cook on the ship, but he never showed up before we left port, so the ten of us take turns. Tonight was mine. I cooked steaks. They didn't turn out too bad.

I can't believe you hate baseball. Why?

Be happy,

Welder Man

PS Neither. I want meat on my sandwich. What do you do in your spare time?

Dear Welder Man,

My intense dislike of baseball goes back to elementary school when I was pitching. Not because I was any good at it, but because it was my turn to pitch. Someone hit a line drive. I don't even remember where it hit me, but it hurt. I've hated it ever since.

See no baseball,

Mom of Five

PS I have five kids. I don't have spare time. I'm kidding a little. After I put the kids to bed, sometimes I take a walk down the lane, especially when the moon's out. I like the dark. You?

I can't believe you don't like peanut butter and jelly. The kids and I live on that. What's meat?

Dear Mom of Five,

The righteous man falleth seven times yet riseth again. I can't believe you're letting one ball keep you from enjoying America's favorite pastime. Tell you what, maybe you can continue to hate baseball in general, but you can fall in love with the Cardinals. How's that?

Be open to baseball,

Welder Man

PS When I'm home, I like to visit my family. I've also been thinking of taking up farming. You mentioned fruit trees. I've been thinking about apples a lot. There's a lot of good information on the Internet, but I want to order books. Unfortunately, USPS doesn't deliver here.

Do you read?

I guess when I get back stateside, I'll have to take you and the kids out for a real meal. I sure hope you are kidding about the meat question. Baseball, I can probably let it slide. (Notice the pun?) But meat? I can't compromise on it. Sorry.

✳

Dear Welder Man,

Okay, you convinced me. I was letting pain dictate my choice. I'll try baseball. What time's the next game? And who am I supposed to root for again?

See I can be taught,

Mom of Five

PS I didn't say we didn't like meat. We just can't afford it. Well, that's not true now. I've actually been making some money lately, but it's not going to last, so I don't want to spend it. So peanut butter and jelly it is. Occasionally we mix it up with macaroni and cheese and hot dogs. Hot dogs are meat. So there, you don't have to compromise.

I love to read, but I don't usually have too much time. I like fantasy. Something that's completely different from the real world. I want to escape and get caught up in fairies and unicorns and pixie dust. And go on a good quest with a man of valor. Or a faun of valor, or whatever.

What do you like to read, other than about apples?

Dear Mom of Five,

You weren't serious about asking about games and times, right? Because you know it's the end of October.

Be serious,

Welder Man

PS Buy yourself some meat. The kids need it. Spend some of your moldy money. Or I'll do it for you. Hot dogs don't count. They're not really meat. Look at the package, they're just nitrates and ground-up plastic parts that fell off the machinery as it was processing steaks and roast. I promise there's no nutrition in hot dogs. You gotta do right by your kids, lady.

I've been consumed with apples lately. I have a new favorite kind, although I've never tasted it. Arkansas Black. Man, you have to look that up. https://www.bing.com/images/search?q=arkansas+black+apple+pic *Aren't they gorgeous? You can't believe how hungry I am for apple pie, apples and caramel, apple dumplings, apple anything, and there isn't an apple left on board the ship. Trust me. I checked.*

So I quit reading about apples and started reading about sharks.

There aren't any sharks on the ship either.

I have seen a couple in the water. Not the ones with big teeth though.

Dear Welder Man,

Sharks in the water?!?!?!?!

You're kidding, right?

Hopefully. I mean, I guess there's probably sharks in the water, but you don't actually see them, right? That sounds dangerous.

Are you going to tell me we can't be friends if I was truly serious about that baseball question? I'm not even sure what I said that was wrong.

See the other person's side,

Mom of Five

PS Your apples are beautiful. You won't believe this, but we actually have Arkansas Blacks around here, and I was just picking some today. They're sour. Just saying. One of the old-timers said that if you put salt on them, they don't taste sour. I haven't tried it. It doesn't even sound good to me.

Now, caramel on the other hand? I think we have that in common.

I haven't had time to make any pies, but I can. And I plan to. Thanksgiving isn't that far away. I think my kids are tired of apples—they're cheaper than meat—but I've been looking at stuffing that has apples, baked apples, and I'm pretty sure I can make 10 apples into the shape of a turkey. I don't think I have to spend any money on Thanksgiving dinner. And it's not moldy, I'm just saving it, because I know what it's like to not have any.

I think you should read about the desert.

Dear Mom of Five,

I wasn't kidding about the sharks, but I said their teeth were little. It's the ones with the big teeth that are scary.

Baseball is over for the year. You just missed it. I wonder if it's on purpose.

Be honest,

Welder Man

PS I've been reading about the desert. It has sand and no sharks. There's no water either, so might be a little hard for me to make a living. Thanks for the suggestion, though.

I tried one of your fantasy books. I couldn't suspend my disbelief long enough to get into it. How do you read that stuff?

I think I'm going back to apples.

Although, I had to delete your email that talked about apple pies, apple dumplings, baked apples, apples and caramel, apple everything, because I am really craving apples right now. Did I mention there are no apples on the ship?

But we have tuna. There's like fifty-seven cans of tuna in the galley pantry. Fifty-seven. Like seriously, if we really want tuna, we can throw a line over the side of the ship and work on getting ourselves some.

Apples on the other hand? No go.

I think I'm going to oversee the packing of the galley next time. Especially if I have to cook.

We do, however, have cinnamon. I thought I might take some tuna and make an apple pie out of it. I'll let you know how it goes.

Dear Welder Man,

I've never watched a game of baseball in my life. I really didn't know the season was over. Although, it kind of makes sense. I guess they don't play in the winter.

I like figure skating.

See the apple pie,

Mom of Five

PS So I have to know, how'd the pie turn out? I was talking to one of the old-timers here, and I was telling him about your tuna pie with cinnamon, and he mentioned that he has a recipe that uses zucchini, and it tastes just like apple pie.

I didn't believe him.

He came back this morning at 5:30, I'm not even kidding about that, and I have to admit that I wasn't dressed when he knocked on the door. But if he thought it was weird that I only stuck my head out, he didn't say.

He gave me his zucchini that's supposed to taste just like apple pie recipe along with two zucchini, and he told me he's coming back tomorrow to ask me how it is. I was going to pick apples today. But I think I'll have to make a pie before I do. Hopefully, mine turns out better than I suspect yours did, although I think we both might be considered a little nuts.

Dear Mom of Five,

If I drop baseball, will you drop figure skating?

How do you feel about bull riding?

Be a rodeo fan,

Welder Man

PS The mightiest oak tree was once a little nut.

I think a little nutty is good. I guess I have to because all the guys on this ship are a little nutty, including me. We have to be.

So, the pie.

Little note about the guys on the ship. If you catch them as soon as they get off work, and they're sober, they're a little pickier about what they'll eat.

By about midnight? They loved it. I'll give you the recipe.

On the other hand, I don't think you should be getting quite that drunk. Not when you're responsible for five children. Never mind about the recipe.

Email me if you're ever in charge of feeding a ship full of sailors and have fifty-seven cans of tuna and no apples, and I'll share.

I will say we're down to forty-nine cans of tuna. And I used half the container of cinnamon. I think it might have been a little much.

I took notes for next time.

How did your zucchini pie turn out? And if you tell me that you had to get your kids drunk in order to get them to eat it, I'm afraid I'm going to have to turn you in.

Dear Welder Man,

Dropping baseball. Dropping figure skating. Dropping bull riding.

How do you feel about curling?

See new things,

Mom of Five

PS I'm a little concerned about life on board the ship and how it might be corrupting you. I guess I thought the whole thing about sailors and alcohol was an old wives' tale.

How drunk did the chef have to be in order to make the apple pie out of tuna?

You are not gonna believe this, but my zucchini pie tasted exactly like apple pie. I'm not even kidding. The man was right. You cannot tell the difference. I would have sworn on a stack of Bibles that that thing was an apple pie with real apples.

I don't want the recipe to get out though, because I've been selling apples. Apples are a lot more expensive than zucchini. If you can make apple pie out of zucchini that tastes exactly like apple pie, why in the world would you buy apples when you can get zucchini for like one-tenth of the price?

So I burned it. The recipe not the pie.

I didn't figure you'd care, because—I'm guessing here—there's no zucchini on the ship either.

Chapter Six

Dear Mom of Five,

> *Man, you're a riot. Curling? That's a good one.*

> *Have you ever jumped out of an airplane?*

> *See the excitement,*

> *Welder Man*

> *PS My parents were killed by a drunk driver. I've never touched alcohol.*

> *I hope you remember how to make it. I can't imagine a zucchini pie would taste like apple. Although, as far as I know, you've never lied to me. I think that's one thing I'm going to have to see to believe. Or taste to believe. So, I owe you and the kids a steak dinner. You owe me a zucchini pie that tastes like apple.*

> *Curling. *shakes head* I think I like you.*

Dear Welder Man,

> *This may surprise you, but I actually have jumped out of an airplane.*

> **me giggling over your stunned silence**

> *Okay, I admit the airplane was on the ground when I jumped out of it.*

> *Have you?*

See no reason,

Mom of Five

PS My ex-husband was an alcoholic. I'm so sorry about your parents. How old were you?

I remember how to make the pie, and I owe you one.

I know I like you.

Dear Mom of Five,

Ha. You got me there for a minute. Anyone who doesn't like baseball couldn't possibly jump out of an airplane.

I have. Jumped out of an airplane. While it was in the air. It wasn't really a planned jump.

Be daring,

Welder Man

PS I'm planning on coming home soon, but I have a job I promised to do, so I won't be in the states long. This time. I know I'll be back by the middle of December. There's a little town in Arkansas called Mistletoe. If you meet me at the only diner in town on Christmas Eve, I'll make sure you get a steak dinner.

Dear Welder Man,

I'm having trouble picturing what a "not planned" jump out of an airplane looks like. Maybe you could give me some details? On the other hand... nvm.

A long time ago, you said your job was dangerous, and I believe you. Ever since then, I've wondered something and am going to ask you now. Why do you do it?

Help me see,

Mom of Five

PS Would you believe that I know where Mistletoe is?

I'll meet you there on Christmas Eve.

Dear Mom of Five,

You know, your question made me think.

I had a pretty easy, pat answer that I was gonna give you, and then something happened that made me think even more and gave me pause, and I thought that maybe it would be okay if I went into a little deeper detail.

First, the thing that happened.

I told you my job is kinda dangerous. It involves fixing things underwater. Kinda complicated for the layman, and it's not that I don't think you can understand, it's just that I would have paragraphs of boring information, because I can really get into it.

Let me say it like this: we go down deep enough and stay down long enough that we need to use oxygen tanks and lines in order to breathe. We fix things, but often we can't see with our eyes. The water may be murky, and it's dark too. Not to mention, you always have something over your eyes, and no matter how clean it is, it's never like looking at something on the surface.

Now, I've been doing this job for over a decade and training the five years before that for it. People say I'm good at what I do. Maybe they're right. I'm the boss on this job, although I'm not the supervisor. If that makes sense.

My best friend in the world, Crew, was my point partner on this dive. We were working down below on this together. There are a lot of things that can go wrong, and you asked why I do it.

When I was younger, I would have said for the money.

Anyway, you have to be careful. There are currents when you're under the water like we were. You can get caught in them, run out of oxygen, and drown.

We did stagger dives, and I left before Crew did. He still had fifteen minutes.

I noticed the tug of the current as I left the job site and came slowly to the surface.

When you're down that deep, you have to rise carefully and slowly, or nitrogen bubbles can form in your blood. It's painful, and it can kill you.

Maybe the current got stronger after I left, I don't know, but Crew got caught in it.

It moved him from the job where we were, and he got hooked on some of the framework we were working on. Visibility was low, and it took a while to get himself unhooked.

He surfaced too fast.

I have him hooked up to oxygen, but what he needs is a pressurized chamber. We don't have it on the ship. We're headed toward port, but it's going to be morning before we're close enough that a helicopter can come to lift him. Might be too late by then.

I'm sitting by his bedside, holding his hand, and thinking about your question.

This could be his last night on earth.

And it could have just as easily been me. He was supposed to go first, but he had a problem with his gear, and I took his place.

It makes you think.

I told you, when I first started, I would have said the money.

Ten years ago, I would have said the challenge, pitting myself against nature and winning.

Five years ago, I would have said the satisfaction of doing a challenging job that not too many people can do and that needs to be done. Someone has to do it, and I can.

Now?

I like the idea of apple trees.

I'm sorry. My buddy's dying, and I showed a little more of my heart than I might've otherwise.

I'm going to ask you a question. Why did you end up alone with five children?

Sincerely,

Welder Man

Natalie sat on the farmhouse porch swing, one foot tucked up under her, one foot gently pushing against the floor, rocking slowly.

Her eyes closed, and the hand that held her phone dropped into her lap.

She said an immediate prayer for Welder Man. It wasn't his name, obviously, but God knew who he was.

She was tired, the kind of good weariness that came after a day of hard manual labor.

She'd been able to quit her job as a telemarketer, focusing on the apple orchard, after talking to Joel, who had told her to go ahead and sell the apples, keeping the money. Obviously, no one else was going to do it. And there was already a stand set up.

The apples were there—the previous owner had taken care of them through the spring and summer.

So were the customers.

So, she'd been spending her days picking apples.

It was a fun job. Hard, tiring, and she would have said, before reading Welder Man's email, dangerous.

About half of the trees in the orchard were dwarf trees. She'd figured that out by looking it up on the internet. The other half were standard-size trees. Which meant she needed to use a ladder in order to pick them.

At least, her children were happy in the orchard while she picked. It was a fun place to play.

They found things to keep them occupied, although Jack and Maggie helped her. Even Ramona picked the drops up, and she'd figured out that they could be used for cider. She found a cider press, there was a cooler in the market stand, and she'd been selling cider and apples.

She had to guess on a few of the varieties, because she hadn't been able to identify them all over the Internet.

Regardless, she could pick upwards of eighty bushels a day. Along with what the children picked, they were close to one hundred bushels each day.

Of course, they didn't pick every day, and picking wasn't the only thing they had to do. She'd learned to drive the tractor. Thankfully, it was small, and they brought the apples down and sorted them, bagged them, and sold them.

After the first week, she'd used up all the bags she'd found in storage in the market under the counter, but by then, she'd had enough money to order bags.

Every day, in every way, she was amazed at what God had done.

Funny, because when she started her correspondence with Welder Man, she was the one who was in dire straits.

She still was…kind of.

Apples weren't going to last forever, and the owner of the house wasn't going to be gone forever either. Still, she was better off. But it sounded like Welder Man was worse.

He'd helped her and hadn't even meant to. Probably. Just gave a little offhand comment that struck a chord in her and changed the direction she was headed.

For all she knew, if he hadn't said that, she'd be married to a man like her ex.

And he'd asked why.

The very least she could do was tell him.

Dear Welder Man,

I've been praying for your friend, Crew, and I hope he made it.

Thanks for telling me about what was going on.

It's kind of weird that I don't even know your name but also kind of nice that I don't even know your name. I think it makes it easier for me, because so many of the blanks that need to be filled in are done with my imagination. I'm not limited by my actual knowledge.

Maybe you feel the same way.

Regardless, your story tugged at my heartstrings, and you have been on my mind as well.

One of the nice things about emailing you is that I felt kind of like I had a clean slate. You didn't know my past.

Of course, I didn't exactly look like an intelligent person when we first met, asking you to marry me having never even met you and having put up a profile on the marriage of convenience site.

So, everything I'm about to tell you will probably not come as a surprise. Not after that.

There's no way to sugarcoat it.

I got pregnant when I was fifteen. I managed to figure out how to go to school and take care of that baby, still living with my mom who was divorced and worked full-time. I did have an older sister, but she was out of the house and I barely saw her.

That wasn't enough. I became pregnant again just a few months after my first baby was born.

I'd gone to school through the first pregnancy, but I just couldn't with the second one. I felt too stupid.

It's one thing to make a mistake. It's another thing to repeat that mistake. And it's an even worse thing when everyone knows that you made a stupid mistake and repeated it.

I didn't want my children to think they were mistakes.

Those were a few hard years, and when I had someone take an interest in me, I moved in with him. I was nineteen. Pregnant again.

I suppose I could give you all kinds of excuses why, after that, I still had two more children.

Nothing makes me look good.

And, if you're still reading, to prove that I don't have a brain, I'll just say that I stayed with my husband even though he was slapping me around. It's when he balled his fist up and hit me that I finally left him. Putting my kids in the car, driving away.

I was scared to death.

I had NO idea of what I was going to do.

So yeah. I faced a lot of judgment. And I didn't want to write what I just wrote. Still don't.

It was kinda nice to talk to someone who didn't know all that about me.

Where I live now, people know I'm poor, people know I have a lot of kids, but I haven't told a lot of people the sordid details.

I'm sure you can see why.

I want to think I'm not that person anymore.

I did learn a few things.

First of all, not to depend on anybody else to make me happy.

Second, not to depend on my circumstances to be happy.

Third, a marriage of convenience appealed to me, because I'm not going to fall in love and get swept off my feet anymore either.

Been there, done that, and have the kids to prove it.

I changed a lot of things since then, and I hope that I'm a good influence for my children from now on. Although, I'm not going to hide my mistakes from them.

I hope Crew feels better.

Why aren't you married?

Sincerely,

Mom of Five

Chapter Seven

*D*enver stood against the rail and watched the sun come up over the Atlantic.

Typically when Mom of Five wrote him, her emails came in early in the morning.

He could never decide whether she wrote them before she went to bed or after she got up.

He hadn't realized she was such a mess.

She hadn't said how old her kids were, but he did assume they were young, which made her really young.

Interesting, though, that she had said she was choosing to be happy and not depending on her circumstances or the people around her. Because the thing that had drawn him to her from the first was her whimsical comment. He could just feel the happiness in it.

At least he could tell her Crew made it to shore. Denver wasn't sure if he was actually going to make it beyond that, but that was more than he was thinking had been going to happen last week.

But the ship was almost at port, and he was going home.

Beyond that and the job he'd scheduled for December, he was

giving serious consideration to staying in Arkansas—moving to the farm he'd bought beside his brother and near his parents.

He hadn't even toured the house. Joel had done everything for him other than sign the papers.

DENVER JOGGED through the drizzle to his father's house.

He had two fathers. The one that had been killed when he was a teenager, and the one that adopted him and his five siblings not long afterwards. Although long enough for them all to be shuffled off to different foster homes.

That example alone—of adopting six older children, all at one time—had impressed Denver, probably more than anything that had happened to him in his life. Beyond the death of his parents.

He would be loyal to Race and Penny until he died, and he would call them Mom and Dad. In his heart, he loved his birth parents too. Both sets of parents resided there, and he considered himself blessed to have double what most people did.

Because he loved his parents, or maybe because he hadn't seen his family in months—the job had taken a month longer than they'd planned—he had driven faster than he should have, and a speeding ticket was tucked in the visor of his pickup.

He was slightly late for Thanksgiving dinner.

Knowing his mom, they were holding it for him.

He stomped his feet and shook himself on the porch. The rain was unending and coming down in sheets.

But it was good to see mountains in the distance and hills and trees, even if they didn't have any leaves on them.

He could smell the turkey from here.

He closed his eyes and breathed deep, feeling the love of his home state sink down into his toes. Man, it was good to be home.

He put his hand on the doorknob and stepped in the door.

A house full of people looked up as the door opened, and he barely had three seconds before people started rushing him. His sisters Journee and Blakely pretty much attacked him at once and hugged him tight, chattering over each other. He had no idea what they were saying, but he nodded anyway, hoping he wasn't agreeing to doing anything really awful.

Like watching curling.

The thought made him smile.

He wondered where she was.

What she was doing.

Eating zucchini pie that tasted like apples with her children?

Maybe she was with her mother. He had thought he wouldn't email her on Thanksgiving, because he didn't want to bother her. But email wasn't really a bother.

He hadn't been sure how she felt about him. Other than she said she liked him. But he liked a lot of people that he didn't want to get any closer to.

He wanted to meet her. He couldn't make any judgments about her over email, but he couldn't bring himself to be more forward. Not when he was on the ship, and not when he had to go back out.

It was fun to email someone and not know their name, or what they looked like, or who they were, and just take their words with no preconceived notions.

He'd never done that before, and it had made his time on the ship go by quickly.

It had definitely given him something to think about.

To dream about.

Of course he'd never seen her, so in his dreams, she looked a lot like his brother's wife. Dark curly hair and sparkling blue eyes. And a perpetual smile on her face.

Not that he'd seen her that often, just once. Other than in church a few times.

But that was enough.

Just as it was enough to know his brother was married to her.

He wouldn't think about her anymore. It's just when he thought about Mom of Five, Natalie's face was the one that came to his mind.

He steeled himself, and with an arm around Journee's shoulder and one around Blakely's, they stepped into the room where the table was set.

Maybe it was a little cowardly of him, but he had a sister buffering him on each side, and that's how he'd face Ethan and Natalie.

Only, as they walked in, Ethan's arms were around Denver's other sister Ruby, and there was no doubt that she was his wife, because Denver just couldn't imagine Ethan kissing any other woman like that.

He was staring. He knew he was, trying to figure out why Ethan obviously wasn't married to Natalie and how he'd gotten the idea that he was.

"Would you please stop staring? It's embarrassing me," Shane said from the foot of the table, where he had stolen an olive from the bowl sitting beside the mashed potatoes.

"Why would that embarrass you? You're not the one doing the kissing," Denver said easily.

His other brother, West set the green beans down on the table. "That's because Shane's never kissed anyone. I don't think he realized people did that kind of stuff with their mouths."

"Mom always said to shut your mouth so you wouldn't catch any flies. I didn't realize I could open it and catch a girl." Shane smirked.

"You just keep thinking like that, bro. Can you say bachelor?" West smirked right back at him.

"Seems to me like you could use a little help on your technique too. I don't see a girl on your arm."

"True. But that's not because I open my mouth and try to catch flies...I mean girls."

Penny came around the table, wiping her hands on her apron before brushing it down and holding her arms out.

"Denver," she said, all the love and care and concern of a mother in her voice. "I'm so happy you're home. Are you here to stay?"

She wrapped her arms around him and squeezed tight. She smelled of cinnamon and apples, and he buried his nose in her hair and breathed in deep, even that smell reminding him of Mom of Five. Apples.

He hoped she was having a good day.

"Good to be home, Mom, but I can't stay. I've got one more job before things shut down for the winter. I promised, and I can't go back on my word."

"I understand," his mother murmured.

"How's Crew?" Race came over with his hand out. Denver kept one arm around his mother and reached out with his right to shake his dad's hand.

"He's gonna make it. He's gonna have some problems, though," Denver said, his voice subdued. It was the risks of the job. They all knew it. But, man, he felt like it was his responsibility. His fault.

He'd gone over and over in his mind the things he could have done to change it. What if he hadn't gone first? What if, when he felt the current, he'd gone back and warned Crew? What if he'd waited?

If he'd waited, he might have run out of oxygen himself.

Still, maybe his mind was too focused on Mom of Five, and it interfered with his work.

He didn't think he'd been thinking about her down below, but she popped in his head at the weirdest times.

He'd never had trouble with that before.

He didn't recall thinking about her while they were working. But he supposed it was possible. He was sure she was there in his head. Funny how certain things would just bring her to mind. A word. A smell. Seeing the dark shadow of a shark. An airplane overhead.

She came to mind, and a smile came to his lips. It was automatic.

"Denver?"

He realized Ethan had been talking to him. "I'm sorry."

Everyone looked sad, like they figured he was still upset about

Crew. He felt a little guilty that he hadn't even been thinking about Crew but about Mom of Five.

"I'm sorry." He tried to look like it. "Would you repeat that?"

"I was saying you've missed some things since you were last back." Ethan looked as proud as a man could be with his arm around Ruby beside him. They made a striking couple.

"I did," Denver said, scratching his head, still not able to figure out where he went wrong. "I knew you got married. But I guess no one actually told me to whom." He figured he didn't need to say who he'd thought Ethan had gotten married to. Obviously, he'd been wrong about it. "Congratulations to you." He grinned at his sister. "Sorry about your luck."

She rolled her eyes. "Our other two brothers already said that."

Denver dropped his arms from around his mother, walking to Ethan and holding his hand out.

They shook, but Denver's mind had been churning, and now he asked, with a sick feeling in his stomach, "I thought..." If Ethan hadn't married Natalie... "Natalie's house was bulldozed," he finally managed to say.

"I wanted to talk to you about that. We can wait until after dinner," Race said from behind him in a deep voice that wasn't unkind but in a tone that Denver had never been able to argue with.

Even now.

"Let's eat while the food is hot." Penny gave him a gentle smile, and he thought her expression said everything was okay, but where his stomach had been jumping on his kidneys before, he now felt a little bit like he was going to throw up.

Dinner lasted forever. They never rushed Thanksgiving, not just because it was a national holiday, or because being thankful was the way to a happy life, according to his parents, but also because it marked the anniversary of when they had first met Race and Penny.

Denver could hardly wait for it to be over.

His palms were sweating, and he tried to push his food around so it looked like he was eating, but everything was as bland and tasteless as rice with no salt.

Finally, the table was cleared off, the dishes were done, and the family had gathered in the living room. It sounded like they were getting ready to play charades, breaking up into teams.

Thankfully, Race and Penny came out of the kitchen after starting the dishwasher, and Denver was waiting for them.

"Dad?"

Race and Penny exchanged a look, which made Denver's stomach drop even more.

"You want to go out on the porch for a few minutes, son?" Race asked, but it wasn't a question. Not really.

Denver opened the door and waited, following his father out.

It was still raining, but not as heavy. The sound of the drops hitting the tin roof normally soothed and relaxed him. Small drops and muted noise that could make anyone fall asleep. But it didn't feel soothing to Denver. Not now.

He'd bought that farm and okayed the demolition of the house that Natalie was living in, because he thought his brother had married her. That she had a home.

He'd been wrong.

He wanted to jump right into the conversation. Maybe ten years ago, he would have.

But part of his job, the job he was really good at, was being patient, eyeing things up, and thinking about them so he did everything right the first time. He might not get a second chance. He didn't rush into a job without making sure everything was lined up perfectly.

So he waited.

Race walked to the far corner post and leaned a shoulder on it, looking out across the yard toward the church as the rain came down. "I talked to Joel some at church just about the time you bought your farm."

"Joel was supposed to be taking care of everything. He told me things were fine. Was there a problem?"

"Not really."

Okay, so his job did prepare him to be patient and to look things over and to make smart decisions. But he was used to working with his hands. Being active.

He took several long strides to the swing, but he didn't sit down. Reaching up, he grabbed a hold of the chain, hanging on it a little and looking out into the dark night.

"Just tell me what happened to Natalie. Please." Dark curly hair and dancing blue eyes flashed through his mind. Along with Ethan's low words that he thought she left her husband because he'd hit her.

She might not have a home.

While he'd been spending the summer sending cute little emails back and forth with some stranger he didn't even know.

That wasn't fair.

He was being hard on himself.

Mom of Five was also a single mom, although she did seem to get into a job that had kept her busy all summer and made her some money. It had something to do with fruit, although she hadn't been specific.

There his lips went twitching up again. Like they had a tendency to do every time he thought of her.

But Natalie.

He didn't even know Natalie. Not really. He'd just seen her once or twice.

He'd liked the way she looked.

He'd never even seen Mom of Five, but he liked the way she acted.

He'd always thought of himself as a one-woman man. He hated this torn feeling, where he felt like his loyalty should be toward Natalie, but it wasn't.

"Well, son." His dad stopped, and the seconds ticked by.

Denver finally turned. "Yeah?"

The rain continued to patter on the roof.

Denver clenched his jaw. "If something happened to her, Dad, I can handle it. Just tell me, okay?"

"She's fine. Her kids are fine." His dad ran a hand through his hair. "That's not the problem. I've…never done this with anyone in my life before. I never thought I would see the day…" His voice trailed off. This drawn-out suspense was driving Denver nuts.

"Dad? You don't usually have such a hard time talking. This must be really bad."

"I'm going to make a suggestion about something, and I know because I'm your father, you're going to take it seriously, and you're going to think about it. And probably, unless I miss my guess, you're going to do it. And I'm just…I know this is the right thing. I know it's what you need to do. But I hesitate to say it."

Denver nodded. "Dad, there's no one in this world I respect more than I respect you and admire you. What you did with us kids? Adopting a pack of teenagers? No one else in the world would do that. There were six of us. You guys wanted us. And you took your job seriously. You guys are amazing. All you have to do is say the word, and you know I'm doing it."

Race had smiled at the beginning of his speech, but by the end, his eyes dropped, and he sighed and looked away. "That makes me feel more than ever that I shouldn't say anything, but I feel it's the right thing to do. I just…I've been praying about it and really feel like God's hand is in this." He shook his head. "It's hard to say that, because I don't really feel like God tells someone else what you should do in your life."

"Tell me, Dad. I'll do it." Denver was confident. His dad would never tell him to do anything that he shouldn't do. Ever.

A little burst of heavier rain hit the tin roof, echoing down the porch. Fifteen seconds later, it slowed back down again.

Finally, Race spoke. "Natalie's okay. She's done okay for herself over the summer. The church has been making sure she's been taken care of, but she needs a dad for her kids, and she deserves a good man." His dad turned to face him full-on. "I think it should be you."

Denver's stomach had started to churn. If his dad had said that to him four months ago, he wouldn't have had a problem with it… but now?

Mom of Five.

No baseball.

No bull riding.

But she jumped out of an airplane. The thought still made his lips want to turn up.

She had sass and spunk and a sense of humor that would make being around her fun.

But as far as he could remember, Race had never asked him for a favor. Not even one time. He couldn't turn him down, even if it meant changing the course of the rest of his life.

He wasn't committed to Mom of Five. He hadn't even told her he liked her, really. Their emails weren't flirty and definitely not suggestive.

She wasn't anything more than a friend. He didn't even know what she looked like.

In the meantime, Natalie had struck him from the first time he'd seen her, and he knew he could help her. Plus, she lived around here, and if that weren't enough, his dad had asked him to.

There was no way he was turning his dad down.

If Natalie would have him, he'd do whatever she wanted.

"I'll go see her. And if she'll have me, I'll do it."

He'd met Mom of Five because of a marriage of convenience.

How ironic that he could lose her the same way.

But he wasn't going tonight. It was Thanksgiving.

And he wasn't going to go tomorrow, either. Wherever Natalie was, whatever she was doing, she could wait one more day while he checked out the farm he'd bought and opened up the house so that it would be fit to live in.

She was probably renting an apartment in Mistletoe, and she'd survived this long; she could manage a few more days until he made his house habitable.

He almost opened his mouth to ask his dad where she was, but there was a heaviness in his chest he just couldn't shake.

It wasn't that he didn't like Natalie, because he did. She was compelling. But he just wasn't a two-woman man, and he had Mom of Five in the back of his head, slowly marching forward throughout the fall as he chatted with her and had started to really like her.

He thought she felt the same about him. He wasn't exactly an expert in that area. He lived his job.

He closed his mouth over the words.

He could give himself a day, maybe two, to come to grips with it.

He needed to send Mom of Five an email.

His stomach dropped and hit the floor with splatter.

What was he going to say?

Ugh.

He didn't even know how to start that. Did she like him? Didn't she? Was she thinking there was going to be more? He sure had hoped so. But he hadn't been in any rush. With him being on the ship, there was nothing he could do anyway. He'd enjoyed their playful emails—innocent and sweet and funny—and sometimes they even talked about deeper spiritual things.

He wanted a woman that he could talk to about anything. Mom of Five definitely fit that bill.

"Son?"

Race's voice stirred him out of his thoughts, and he jerked his head up. He'd completely forgotten that Race was even there.

"Yeah?"

"Forget about it. I can see it's upset you. And I don't want you doing this out of loyalty or a feeling of guilt or feeling like you have to repay me for anything. You know you don't."

"You know I owe you more than I could ever repay." Those words didn't come out harshly or bitterly, although they could have. Maybe in someone else. Denver didn't feel that way at all. "I'm more grateful than I can ever say for what you and Penny did for me. And for my siblings. You saved us. Who knows where we would have ended up or what would have become of us if you hadn't stepped in and done what you did? You gave us a stable home, provided everything that we could need and most of our wants too. You picked up where our parents left off, and you did an amazing job. Basically, you sacrificed your lives for us. How could I not think I owe you?"

He stared at his dad as Race's eyes filled with tears.

Denver's heart lurched. He didn't want to see his dad cry. Just didn't. But he couldn't look away. He couldn't pretend it wasn't happening.

"You've never said anything like that before," Race said, his voice forced. The tears that had pooled in his eyes had not spilled over, but a muscle in his jaw ticked in and out, and the knuckles that wrapped around the porch pillar were white.

"I'm sorry. I should have." Denver turned, dropping his hand from the porch swing chain and striding toward his dad until he was leaning against the opposite porch pillar with the opening of the stairs between them. "I guess today's Thanksgiving, and if I were reflecting on things I was thankful for, you and Penny are number one on that list. You share that spot with my birth parents. The difference is I was given to them. You chose me. And my siblings. Thank you."

Denver cursed his stupid inability to ever articulate the things he should. And let the people around him know how much he appreciated them.

"I love you, Dad." He didn't say that nearly enough.

He supposed he'd always felt it was more important to show it. Show it by, when his dad gave him advice, or made a suggestion, or requested something of him, even if it was something that was so off the wall that anyone in their right mind would totally dismiss it, he would do it. Because he loved his dad. And he didn't just say that, not nearly as much as he should, but he showed it.

"I love you too, son." Race stepped forward, and Denver met him halfway. They wrapped their arms around each other and held on tight for a long time.

Finally, Race pulled back, holding on to his shoulders. "Pray about it. Don't do it for me. I'm not asking for me. As crazy as it seems to me, I feel that's what the Lord would have you do. But you have to think that, too. If you do it, don't do it for me. Do it because that's what you know God wants."

Chapter Eight

Denver sat at the top of the waterfall, inches away from the water rushing past, his feet hanging down over the side.

When he'd been a teenager, just after he got his driver's license, and when he'd started training to be both a diver and welder, this had been his favorite place to come.

It was an hour away from his parents' home but worth the drive.

The Ozarks were filled with beautiful places, although he couldn't see the beauty tonight.

It was dark.

And cold.

The spray from the water made the air damp.

There were plenty of uncomfortable times on board the ship. Dark. Damp. When he'd been wet from the spray.

Nothing new.

At least this water wasn't salty. Salt water made his clothes stiff and his skin dry and scratchy.

Despite the dark and cold, it wasn't hard to feel what always stirred him about this place.

It wasn't just the natural beauty and the power of the falls. It was just a stream but still dangerous with the wet rocks where one could slip and fall to their death.

It happened every summer once, sometimes several times.

Denver reached out and put his hand in the ice-cold water rushing past.

It was the way his brain felt right now, rushing toward the abyss, in a few seconds going over the edge out into space in a free fall.

Maybe that was a little dramatic. That's how he felt, just unable to stop his thoughts.

Why, Lord? Why did I have Mom of Five all summer, all fall?

Why did she send me that email? Of all the men in the world that could have gotten that email, why was it me? Why me, God, if you weren't going to use it to bring us together?

Why couldn't you have warned me not to get my emotions involved?

He pulled his hand out of the water, numb.

He held his phone in his other hand, an email written to Mom of Five.

He hadn't sent it. Probably wasn't going to.

Using his left hand, he looked at his phone.

Dear Mom of Five,

I couldn't believe how much you trusted me when you sent me that last email.

All the hard things you've been through, as messy as it was…you could have hidden it. You could have pretended. But you were honest with me, and I admire that.

I admire your determination to keep your kids.

The whole time I was reading, I thought about the things we talked about over the past few months, and I realized how much you'd grown from what you were to what you are now.

I was impressed.

I wanted this email to say something completely different, but I'm writing what I don't want to.

I don't think I told you about my parents. It's a long story, and I don't think it matters anymore.

Just know that I owe my dad a lot.

Today, he asked me to do something, something hard. Something I don't really want to do. Something that's going to keep me from doing what I wanted.

This is me taking a deep breath, because I'm about to say something that's risky.

In this email, I originally wanted to ask you if you wanted to meet. Not on Christmas Eve, like we planned in a whimsical kind of way. But seriously meet.

All the emails this summer... I looked forward to every one. I've read them over and over. I want to meet you. And not just in an "I want to see you" kind of way.

But in an "I want to see if there can be something between us" kind of way.

I want to be more than friends.

But something happened tonight that makes that impossible.

I told you I owe my dad. I owe my dad my life. I owe him more than I can ever repay.

He's the kind of man who never asks for anything.

I'd give him anything he wanted, but he never asks for favors, he never asks me to do anything, he just loves me the way I am.

I just want to do something, you know?

Then tonight. Tonight, for the first time that I can ever remember, my dad asked me to do something.

I couldn't tell him no. I still can't.

But that means I had to write this email to you. It means everything I wanted, everything I hoped would happen between us, can't now.

Sorry. I wish... I wish things had worked out differently. I wanted things to work out differently. I thought, was one hundred percent sure that God was going to work things out differently.

But he didn't, and now I have to do what I said I was going to do, and so, maybe you don't feel the same, but I'll never know.

This is goodbye. I can't be emailing you when I have to marry someone else.

I wish you the best. The very best. Thank you for the fun, for the laughs, for the deep discussions... for everything.

Sincerely,

Denver (Welder Man)

DENVER'S THUMB hovered over the send button. Should he?

He took a breath and clicked his phone off.

God, why?

He hated this torn feeling. Hated knowing he needed to do what his dad wanted him to, and part of him wanted to do that too. And beyond the fact that his dad wanted him to marry Natalie, that he was sure that was what God wanted, he wanted it as well.

He'd been intrigued with Natalie from the first time he saw her. He knew his dad wouldn't ask him to marry someone who didn't have character, and there was most definitely an attraction there for him anyway.

It wasn't that it was such a hardship. It was just...

He let his heart get tangled up in feelings for Mom of Five.

Even if he just had a little bit of time, he could get over it. It just wasn't something that he could turn on and off like a switch.

The water ran beside him, never ending.

So much of his life had been about water.

It fascinated him. But also, looking out over the surface, he never knew what lay beneath.

Kind of like people.

He couldn't tell his dad today that someone had started to take over his heart. Just couldn't do it.

It was under the surface. His dad couldn't see that.

Part of him wanted to just leave. He didn't have to stay. He didn't have to say anything to Natalie.

He could go back to his dad right now, tell him he changed his mind, and his dad wouldn't be angry and wouldn't think any less of him.

Even though he'd given his word and said he'd do it. His dad would understand. He knew it. Sure as he was sitting here.

But he couldn't do it. Just couldn't.

He couldn't send that email to Mom of Five either.

Maybe, after he talked to Natalie, things would be easier.

Or maybe Mom of Five would send him an email. Maybe she'd say she found someone. And he wouldn't have to.

Maybe that was the coward's way out.

It wasn't the way he usually chose—usually he was a very take-charge kind of person.

But he didn't want to close the door on Mom of Five.

Maybe Natalie wouldn't accept his marriage proposal.

It wasn't right to keep anyone on a string, like a backup, like if Natalie didn't take him, maybe Mom of Five would.

That's not what he wanted either.

Maybe some other time. He'd send the email some other time.

He looked out into the black night, into the deep, inky emptiness, filled with the sound of rushing water, and thought of the verse in James—"a double-minded man is unstable in all his ways."

Unstable like water.

He pulled his feet up and stood, swaying just a minute until he caught his balance, a little off in the dark.

He knew in his heart what the right thing to do was. His heart just really didn't want to do it.

Lord. Help my actions to be right. Help my heart to follow. Amen.

A simple prayer. Sometimes, they were the best kind. He looked again at the rushing water.

Only a little piece of him wished that he were that free.

Chapter Nine

Natalie wiped a stray hair that had fallen out of the bandanna she had tied over the top of her head back with the crook of her arm, not wanting to touch her face with the rubber gloves she had on. She leaned her elbows on the seat of the toilet and sighed.

The stench of feces hung in the air. The laughter and calling of her children drifted down the hall. Kole splashed happily in the bathtub beside her, his toys floating around and his baby babbling happy and content.

She'd never replaced a toilet before.

It wasn't that she couldn't afford to pay a plumber.

She had sold far more apples than she ever thought she would, and she had a nice little nest egg in the bank.

But this house wasn't going to be their home forever, and apple season was over.

However, if the owner of the house stayed away, there were Christmas trees. At least 40 acres of them. When people had come to buy apples, they had often asked her if she was selling Christmas trees this year.

Apparently, it was tradition for a lot of them to come to this farm and buy them.

They'd told her that they used to get hayrides and have bonfires and roast hot dogs and there were even a few years where there was a corn maze and a shelled corn pit for the kids to play in.

They'd told her that back before the lady of the house had died five years ago, she'd made crafts, Christmas decorations, wreaths, and done special orders.

Ideas—fun ideas, crafty ideas, crazy ideas—ran all through her head. She could totally do that.

Except the house wasn't hers.

Selfishly, she'd hoped the owner would stay away until the end of the apple season. And he had. God's hand at work, probably, but now, she kind of wished he'd stay away until after Christmas.

She planned to go down later and sit at the market and see if anyone came to buy a tree.

She hadn't done any advertising, didn't even have any signs up. But if people came, she'd sell them trees. There were a bunch of old, rusty handsaws in the back shed. When she'd seen them—as she was looking for more apple bags—she'd supposed they'd given out handsaws and people had cut their own Christmas trees down.

Hopefully that's what happened, because she certainly didn't have a clue of how to cut down a Christmas tree.

But if she could change a toilet, she could cut down a Christmas tree.

She was betting the tree would smell better.

This bathroom had always stunk a little, and yesterday after fixing the clogged toilet for like the millionth time since they'd moved in, she'd noticed a small wet spot disappearing under the ratty linoleum that abutted the base of the toilet. Upon a little further inspection, she'd realized it was leaking.

YouTube was her friend, and rather than pay a plumber, she decided she was going to do it herself.

She turned the water off, flushed the toilet and got all the water out of it, took the screws out, and wiggled it to make sure it was loose.

That's when things really started to smell bad.

She suspected that all those times the toilet plugged and overflowed with not so clean toilet water in it, the water had run down through the cracks in the linoleum and seeped into the subfloor.

Something was telling her that this was going to be a bigger job than just changing the toilet.

Now that she started it, she could hardly not finish it.

A couple of her kids seemed to be arguing in the hall. As soon as she got this toilet off, she was going to have to go mediate that. Although, by that time, they'd probably be in tattling on each other.

She wiggled the toilet—heavier than it seemed—grabbed a hold of it like they demonstrated in the YouTube video, and tugged.

It moved but didn't come up. Something was stuck.

Kole threw a toy. It hit the side wall, barely missing her head.

She gave her baby a baleful look. "No. Don't throw."

He smiled his gap-toothed smile at her and laughed. She had to smile back. He took another toy in his hand and splashed it on the water. Goodness. At least he didn't throw it.

She'd taken the screws out like the video had showed her, so the toilet must just be hooked on something. She tugged harder.

Kole, splashing in the tub, rolled over on his belly. He rolled a little too fast and cracked his head on the side of the tub, just as Natalie yanked harder on the toilet and whatever it was catching on popped loose.

She flew backwards and fell on her back. The toilet landed on top of her—a position she'd never thought she'd be in with a toilet.

Kole started to scream. From bumping his head, she assumed, although maybe it was from seeing his mother attacked by a toilet. With a one-year-old, who knew?

The door, already partly open, flew open the rest of the way, banging back against the wall. Three of her other children came running in.

Jack and Maggie were yelling, each of them trying to say what their side of the story was, while Ramona was screaming as blood dripped off her forehead and down her cheek.

She supposed it was one of those Murphy's Law things. It couldn't just be one thing that happened. It had to be a whole slew of them.

The blood concerned her the most, but she eyed it with the experience of a mom of five. It was a head wound but wasn't gushing, and there wasn't even a knot. Ramona would be fine, despite the screeching screams that almost drowned out her siblings' shouted argument.

Natalie sighed, dropping her head back down on the floor and staring up at the ceiling, a small smile on her face—at the ridiculousness of the situation—despite her weariness.

The space was small; she was going to have to crawl out from underneath the toilet, since she didn't have enough room to roll it off her.

Thankfully, it wasn't any heavier than a kid.

Suddenly the screaming around her stopped.

She let it go for about two seconds, then raised her head to make sure that Kole was still in the bathtub and hadn't drowned. His screams had been just as loud as his siblings, adding to the cacophonic dissonance.

But he was there in the tub. Two chubby little hands hooked over the edge, and his big brown eyes wide open, staring at the doorway.

Now that her head was up, she could see a big shadow in the doorway. A person?

Her eyes turned. A man.

Suddenly the toilet wasn't nearly heavy enough, and she wished she could sink through the floor.

Her hands felt clammy, and her throat closed up.

Chapter Ten

*D*enver.

Ethan's brother. She'd only met him once, but he'd seemed so confident and sure. The kind of man who would never look twice at someone as messed up as she was.

She'd never even talked to him, other than to say hello. There had been no reason to.

They would never run in the same circles. Although his brother was her neighbor, so it seemed reasonable that she would see him occasionally.

The thing was, when she emailed Welder Man, Denver's face was what she saw.

Probably she'd had more fun than she should have emailing a complete stranger. She'd liked him and enjoyed their correspondence, but since she didn't know what he looked like, she had to conjure something up.

It was Denver's face.

Not smart on her part, because now he stood over top of her, his arms crossed, his eyes narrowed, a look of confusion creasing his brows.

Come to think of it, what was he doing in her house?

Her eyes shot open wide, and she yanked herself out from underneath the toilet, which fell down onto the linoleum floor with a clank and a clop.

She scrambled to her feet. Could he be the owner?

She couldn't think of any other reason why he'd be in the house. Unless he knocked and they didn't answer. Maybe...

"Do you want a Christmas tree?" she asked, unable to keep the hope out of her voice.

Please, please, God, please let that be what he wants.

But his brow shot up, and his eyes widened while his mouth opened. "A what?"

Okay. There were times in her life where she wished she could just push the pause button, so she could have a little bit of time to catch up to everyone else. This was one of those times. She wanted to be able to push pause, freeze everyone else while she brushed herself off, maybe even changed her clothes because it really stunk in here, and she had just been lying on the floor, and thought about what she wanted to do.

Or maybe, even give her some time to get over the acute embarrassment that contracted her chest until it felt like her ribs were being sucked in, strangling her esophagus.

But life seldom worked the way she wanted it to, and so she took a deep breath, giving her that much time to collect herself, before she made herself meet his penetrative blue eyes.

"A Christmas tree. People use them at Christmas time in their homes. They put decorations on them and—"

"I know what a Christmas tree is. Why would you think I want one?"

He looked around the bathroom. Kole's head had slowly sunk down the edge of the tub so that only his eyes showed above the rim, his naked butt sticking in the air, almost as high as his head. Ramona was still dribbling blood and looked scared and scary at the same time, if that were possible, with the blood trail down her face. Jack and Maggie were holding each other's hands, and where three minutes ago they had been mortal enemies intent on getting the other one in trouble, they were now fast friends and looked like they would stand shoulder to shoulder against Satan himself. She thought she might see Sky, her two-year-old, hunched down in the hall, peeking between Denver's legs, but she wasn't going to drop her gaze to find out.

"Do people normally show up *here* and ask for Christmas trees?" Denver put a slight emphasis on the word "here."

It made her feel stupid. This, of course, was not the first time in her life that she felt stupid. But it was never a good feeling. Obviously.

And while there were times in her life where it made her duck her head, hunch her shoulders, and walk away ashamed, she didn't exactly have that luxury. The only way out was the doorway he was standing in.

Not to mention she was not going to walk away from her children.

And she wasn't going to let him make her feel ashamed of herself, not in her own house.

Wait. This wasn't her house.

Still, she wasn't going to be ashamed, much. Her eyes did drop. She studied the toilet that lay like a sacrifice at her feet.

Okay, maybe she was ashamed.

A little. But she wasn't going to lose her sense of humor.

She lifted her chin and looked him in the eye. "There are forty acres of Christmas trees on this farm. And yes, I was expecting people to show up and want to buy some today."

"You sell them from your bathroom?"

His face hadn't even twitched. While she had the wildest urge to laugh hysterically. Probably the nervousness and embarrassment and just general wishing-she-was-anywhere-but-here feeling coming out.

If it was possible for her to notch her chin up one more

centimeter, she did so and lifted what she hoped was a regal brow. "If necessary."

He jerked his head ever so slightly at her answer, then his eyes fell to the toilet. "You're repurposing that? A cash register maybe?"

She crossed her arms over her chest and pushed her shoulders back. "As a matter of fact..." She tried to figure out how she could actually repurpose a toilet into a cash register, and she'd have to Google it later, but she was pretty sure that it was physically impossible to turn a toilet into a cash register. She couldn't make that believable, no matter how regal she made herself. "No. I'm not."

"A credit card scanner?"

"No."

"You're building a job johnny, and you're borrowing parts?" She thought she saw his tongue maybe push out his cheek a little. Was he trying not to smile?

The rest of his face was dark though, almost glowering, and she thought not.

"The toilet was leaking, so I'm fixing it."

"Do you have a replacement ready to install?"

Her lips pressed together. She hadn't really even thought of it. All she thought about was getting the old one out, since it was leaking. Not to mention it overflowed last night, and she wanted to get everything cleaned up as fast as she could.

"I was going to get that. As soon as I got this out."

"Oh. You wanted to measure the hole first?" This time, she was pretty sure that he was mocking her.

Which made her angry.

"This is my first time. Do you have experience?"

He blinked. She appreciated that crack in his armor. Like it really wasn't every day someone asked him if he had experience in changing toilets.

Finally, a little smile hovered at the edge of his mouth. Maybe he decided to relax. Or maybe that was wishful thinking on her part.

Whatever it was, his face eased. "If you want me to do it for you, just say so."

"I want you to do it for me," she said automatically. She wasn't gonna turn down an offer of help. If all she had to do was say a sentence, yes sir. She was on it.

He coughed out a laugh. "That was quick."

"Not gonna turn down an offer of good help."

"How do you know it's gonna be good?"

She gave the prone toilet a baleful glance. "Better than mine."

He stepped forward, his hand out. "Maybe we should start with introductions. I'm Denver. And I own this house."

Okay. She wasn't sure what that meant. Was he trying to make her feel bad for being here? He had given her permission. It wasn't like it was a big shock for him to come home and see her. He was the one who hadn't told anyone he was coming.

She was supposed to have a notice, which was what Joel had said. She decided to be direct. Pulling her gloves off, she held her hand out and grabbed his.

She met his eyes without flinching. "I'm Natalie, and I remember you from earlier this summer. You're Ruby's brother."

"That's right. I remember you too."

She felt like there was more in his words than what he was saying. Maybe because of the look in his eye, but she could match that. She'd seen him and not been able to get him out of her head.

His face anyway. It was attached to Welder Man, though.

She needed to shake that.

"So did someone hire you to replace the toilet for me?" he asked kind of hesitantly, like he was trying to figure out how to ask her what she was doing in his house but just couldn't find the words.

"No." She said the word slowly and tried to think of how to say what needed to come next. Obviously, at least to her, he wasn't expecting her to be in his house.

Why not?

No point in letting the confusion drag on. "Your friend Joel approached me at church. It must have been right after you bought this place, because it was right before my house was set to be bulldozed. The one I was living in. Which is the one that was at the end of the property that had termites and was condemned?" She felt like she was rambling a little, but she wanted to make sure he was following her.

"Yes. I knew about the bulldozing. I have to apologize. I didn't know you were still living in it. I thought..." He shoved a hand in his pocket and looked away, like he didn't want to say what he was going to say, and it felt like he ended up saying something completely different. "I thought you moved somewhere else. I wouldn't have let it happen, if I'd known."

"It needed to be done. The house was condemned. And, like I was saying, Joel approached me at church and said that the owner of the house, which I didn't realize was you, was going to be gone, and that I was free to stay here for as long as I wanted, and that I would have plenty of notice before the owner came back."

She bit her lip, because she knew she needed to make an offer to move out, and she didn't want to. She'd been lured into thinking that this was...not permanent but a long time away from when she'd have to leave.

Obviously, her time was up, and she needed to find something else. She needed to be thankful for the time they'd been able to spend here. They'd had a great time over the apple season harvest, had made some money, and now it was time to move on.

"I didn't know you were still living there."

She waved her hand, convinced he was serious. He really didn't know, and he felt bad.

Interesting.

She supposed any normal person would feel a little bit guilty about displacing a single mom with five small children. Especially when he was confronted in a small bathroom with them, as Denver was now.

"I was telling you about Joel. He had offered the house and said I could live in it. He also said I could sell your apples. I hope that was okay? I hadn't heard anything about you coming back yet, so I just assumed that wasn't happening. I was getting ready to sell Christmas trees. Obviously." She grinned, embarrassed, and she added that last bit, hoping that he maybe would say something like, "Well, since you're already preparing for the Christmas trees, want to hang out until after Christmas?"

Only if she did that, obviously she'd be here with him.

That wouldn't work.

Oh, and she was in the biggest bedroom, which she assumed he'd want for his.

The old farmhouse had six bedrooms. Two of them were empty since she had doubled up her children. Still, she needed to brush her hands off and face this.

Denver seemed to be starting to understand. "Joel got called out west for his job. He'd told me the house was taken care of when he left a message but hadn't said by who. I didn't worry about it."

His tone said maybe he should have.

Well, that explained why Joel hadn't told her Denver was coming back.

She stuck her jaw out. "I'm sure you know, since I wasn't expecting you, we can't be out today. However, I'm sure I'm in your room, since I'm in the biggest bedroom."

He started to speak, but she held her hand up.

"If you take care of this toilet, I can get started immediately on looking for a place to live. I have a little bit more money now thanks to your apples, which I can split with you if you want..." *Please say no. Please say no.*

"You did all the work. Keep it." He opened his mouth to say more, but she started in before he could.

"Thank you. So, like I said, it shouldn't be too hard for me to find a place."

She had no idea what she was going to do. Go back to her telemarketing job probably. The thought caused a feeling like a heavy, scratchy blanket to fall over her. She tried to shove it aside. She'd do whatever job she needed to do in order to support herself and her family.

"And I can be out of here. Hopefully soon."

She turned to wash her hands in the sink, since she couldn't step forward like she wanted to and make a regal exit, because he was blocking her way. Plus, she had one child on the floor with a bloody head and another child in the bathtub who was about to start crying at any moment because he was cold. And two others who looked like they were ready to attack the man who had the power to throw her out *right now*.

She needed to intervene.

Regal just wasn't in her vocabulary or her life.

"Would you excuse me? I need a towel." She reached past his shoulder to grab the towel off the rack on the wall.

She should have waited for him to move. She didn't need to know he smelled like hazelnut and the outside, with the faintest wisp of coffee, an enticing scent that immediately conjured up thoughts of Welder Man.

Nuts.

He was part of the reason she'd decided to change the toilet. To stop thinking about him. He hadn't emailed, which hadn't been totally surprising since it was Thanksgiving.

He'd mentioned he was going home, so maybe he was occupied with other things.

She tried not to let it bother her, and it really didn't, other than she kinda started thinking that they were friends. Nothing more, of course. But someone to laugh with and talk to.

She'd been successful, or maybe just when one has a toilet lying on top of one, it was hard to think of anything else, for any normal person, anyway, but now...Denver's scent just brought another man to mind.

She was nuts.

He had moved, and she brought the towel back, sticking it

between her legs so she could grab her baby under the arms and lift him out, pulling the plug so the water could drain.

"Ramona, I see the spot on your head. Come with me. After I get some clothes on Kole, I'll take care of that. I'm pretty sure you're going to be okay since it's not bleeding anymore." She looked at her two oldest children. "Whoever's fault it was, it doesn't really matter. Both of you apologize to your sister because I'm sure neither one of you meant to make her head bleed. Then apologize to each other and try to be more careful."

She'd been doing this long enough she could pretty much figure out what had happened. If not specifics, generalities. It wasn't the way she would normally handle it, but she didn't usually have a man standing in the bathroom with her while she tried to, either.

She smiled at Kole, because it was impossible not to with him looking at her with his crazy-tooth grin and white blond hair, thinking the whole world was just a big joke.

Maybe at one year old, it was.

It didn't change much when a person hit twenty-three, either.

"You think you're going to have a minute to talk to me at some point?" Denver's voice interrupted her thoughts as she stood Kole on the floor and toweled his body off.

"I thought that's what we just did." She tilted her head and looked up at him, her hand still moving. She needed to shift her mind from Christmas trees to rentals and finding a job.

"You talked." He tilted his head a little. "Do I get a chance?"

She stilled, her mouth opening. Then she closed it. He was right. She had waved him off and then never given him a chance. No wonder he hadn't moved. He was probably mad at her.

She wrapped the towel around Kole and picked him up, taking a minute to nestle her nose in his neck and blow raspberries on his soft skin. He giggled and screamed and kicked his legs and arms, and she did it again. Then she looked up at Denver.

"I'm sorry. You're right. I guess I just shifted my brain into a different gear and took off in overdrive."

"So you're a mechanic?" he asked, like that had anything to do with anything.

She shook her head. "My dad was." Not that she was around him that much after he walked out on her mom.

Denver lifted his head in acknowledgment. Then he stepped back, allowing her to exit the bathroom.

She stopped when she reached him at the doorway. "Can I have five minutes, please? I'll get Kole and Ramona taken care of, and I'll be ready to sit and listen to whatever you have to say."

"Fair enough. I'll wait downstairs at the kitchen table."

Their eyes met, and neither of them moved for a minute.

Something odd, something like she'd felt earlier that summer when she'd met Denver for the first time, happened in her stomach. A slightly painful sensation as it constricted.

Her throat went dry too, and in her mind, she pictured his hand, big and calloused, swallowing hers as they shook just a few minutes ago.

Another sensation, one oddly familiar, slid through her head. She felt like she'd seen him before. Not just when she'd met him, but some time. Déjà vu maybe, not that she even really knew what that meant. Just she felt like she'd been with him before.

She shook her head, tightened her grip on Kole, and walked to his bedroom, her kids trailing behind her.

Chapter Eleven

Denver sat at the big wooden kitchen table, his hands clasped, twiddling his thumbs. It was his house; he should get some food out and offer it to her, except nothing in here was his.

He'd been shocked to see a familiar vehicle in the driveway, but he hadn't placed it as Natalie's. He just knew he'd seen it before.

It was more that he wasn't expecting to see anything. As he pulled in, it was obvious someone was living here.

A quick call to Joel had gone to voicemail, but he assumed his friend had given Natalie permission.

She didn't seem like the type of person who would lie about it. She'd used Joel's name.

It didn't matter. Whether she had permission from Joel or not, Denver didn't care.

He'd just been surprised.

He hadn't stayed here last night, hadn't even come to see it, because he figured there'd be a ton of work to do after it sat empty for so long while he was on the job.

And maybe he was procrastinating. He'd been sure as soon as

Race spoke that marrying Natalie was definitely God's will. He'd never been more sure of anything.

But sometimes, although he knew what he should do, he just wasn't all in.

How was he going to say this to her, anyway?

He didn't want her to know that there was a part of him that wasn't ready to fully commit.

If it hadn't been for Mom of Five, it would be a completely different story.

He hadn't sent her an email last night.

She probably didn't expect him to email her on Thanksgiving anyway.

He still hadn't figured out what he was going to say.

If Natalie turned him down, he might not have to say anything.

He wasn't going to hope for that. He would do what Race wanted, because he owed and respected Race. Race was the wisest man he knew, and if Race suggested that he do this, he was going to assume that was after Race had considered it and decided it was best for everyone involved.

Plus, he was sure it was what he was supposed to do.

He walked to the other side of the kitchen. The counters were wiped clean, and everything was in its place. The dishes were washed and put away, and there was nothing but a spoon in the sink.

She'd said something about Christmas trees.

How was he gonna sell Christmas trees?

He could do it for the next week. But what about the week he had to be gone?

He walked back across the kitchen to the door that he'd come in. It went out to a mudroom.

He hadn't even been the whole way through his house.

He'd seen pictures online but hadn't really cared.

It'd been enough to know that it was beside Ethan's farm and close to his parents and in the most beautiful country he'd ever seen, the foothills of the Ozarks in Arkansas.

He had no idea why anyone would want to live anywhere else.

He heard footsteps coming downstairs, and he walked back over to the table, standing behind a chair rather than sitting down. For some reason, he just felt restless.

Nervous.

Of course he felt nervous. He was about to propose marriage. He rubbed his hands together. Not really marriage, like there were feelings involved, although... When he looked at Natalie, something stirred inside of him. Something good.

Looking at her made him feel good.

And...something like anticipation made his heart beat faster. He didn't know why.

She was funny. Lying on the floor underneath a toilet. Calm in all that chaos. There was blood and babies crying and toilets flying...she handled it all like a pro and with a little grin.

If she were a welder, she would be the kind of welder he'd want beside him. Calm and able to think on her feet. Or under a toilet.

Yeah, he could work with someone like Natalie. Easily.

His eyes were glued on the doorway, and he could see down the hall as she came down the stairs and directed four of her children toward a different room, speaking low so that he could hear her voice but didn't know what she said.

She came back into view, her chin up, but she didn't seem to know what to do with her hands. She rubbed them together, then put them in her pockets.

"I know it's your house, but I can get you a cup of coffee? Water? I have sweet tea in the refrigerator as well."

"It wouldn't be home if you didn't have sweet tea. I'll take a glass."

She moved gracefully to the refrigerator and pulled out a pitcher of tea.

His eyes followed her as she went to the cupboard and got two glasses.

Interesting that both Mom of Five and Natalie had worked with fruit this fall. He hadn't realized that. Mom of Five and Natalie seemed to have some things in common. Maybe that's why he seemed pulled toward both of them.

Still, he didn't like the feeling of being tugged in two different directions. He certainly wouldn't have let any feelings get involved with Mom of Five at all—in fact, he wouldn't have been emailing her —if he'd known Race was going to say what he did about Natalie.

She filled the glasses and set the pitcher back in the refrigerator. When she returned to the table, she put her hand on a chair, then gave him an inquiring look. "Are you going to sit down?"

"I was waiting on you."

She chose the opposite end of the table from him. He wasn't sure what that meant.

Should he just pop the question? Did one get down on one's knee when one was proposing a marriage of convenience?

He should have emailed Mom of Five and asked her. He almost laughed at the thought. She hadn't gotten down on one knee to proposition *him*.

He needed to stop thinking about her.

It's just that for so long he had been and hadn't thought anything about it.

He pushed his doubts aside. The sooner he got this over with, the sooner he'd know what the rest of his life would look like. Or what it wouldn't look like.

"So, you guys have been in here for a couple months?"

"Since the end of summer, yes. The beginning of August, I think, is when we moved in."

"I see."

Her fingers twisted together. "If you're mad about that, I'm sorry. I really thought you knew. Joel said—"

He put a hand up. She stopped.

"Don't worry about it. It's fine. Joel didn't tell me, but I would have absolutely been fine with it. In fact, if I'd known that you were here, I might have done things a little differently."

If he had known that Natalie wasn't married, he definitely would have done things differently. He couldn't change the fact that he wouldn't have been home, though.

He'd made good money this summer though. Deep-sea welding was the best money around for a guy like him. Someone who didn't want to be stuck behind a desk all day and wanted to work with his hands.

Couldn't beat it.

Except, he was ready to quit. Not quit necessarily, because he didn't like to think of himself as a quitter, but ready to move on.

He hadn't been joking with Mom of Five. He'd definitely become an apple guy, and he was ready to be a farmer.

"You're raising your children by yourself?" It wasn't the best way to open this conversation, but he didn't know what else to say.

Her face scrunched a little like she wasn't sure what that had to do with anything. "Yes."

She wasn't helping by offering nothing.

"Where's the dad?"

She hesitated.

She had every right to push up and stomp away from the table. Or, at the very least, to tell him to mind his own business. Man, he wasn't doing so hot.

But she did neither, taking a couple of breaths and looking thoughtful.

He thought of Mom of Five and the last email she'd sent. He hadn't even answered after she'd pretty much bared her heart. He hadn't known what to say.

He felt bad about that now. Especially if his next email was going to be an announcement that he was getting married. Or, since there was no waiting period in Arkansas, he could be married by this evening.

"He's gone."

Two words. He tried to think of a question he could ask that would start a natural conversation. It might prove awkward to be married to someone he couldn't talk to.

Mom of Five had been so easy... He stopped that thought. He would not think of her anymore. He would not compare Mom of Five and Natalie again.

"Well, I guess we'll just cut to the chase then."

"If you're trying to think of an easy way to tell me that I need to move out, you can stop wasting your time. I'll move out as soon as I can."

"I'm not trying to ask you to move out. I'm trying to ask you to marry me."

Well. That was one way to do it.

Based on the expression on her face, probably not the best way.

Her mouth hung open, her eyes had gotten wide, and she spilled her tea.

Liquid spread across the table, and he was glad she chose the seat farthest from him. She jumped up, without saying anything, and grabbed a dish towel out of the drawer, coming back and blotting at the spilled liquid.

He felt like he should get up and do something, but she had it under control, so he waited until she finished, grabbed the washrag to wipe the table, rinsed the washrag out, and then took her glass to the sink and set it down before coming back and sitting down.

Seemed to him like it took an awful long time to clean up a simple spill.

Maybe she was thinking.

"I guess I can assume you're not joking?"

"I'm serious."

"That's...weird." She lifted her brows as though daring him to contradict her.

"I said it badly. I'm sorry. I'm nervous."

"I can't tell," she said with a small laugh.

"Really?" Maybe he'd been hiding it too well. Maybe he should let a little of his emotion show, so she'd know he was what? Human? Not scary? Was she afraid of him? "I won't hurt you."

"I know who your parents are. I'm pretty sure that's true."

He noticed that she didn't reassure him completely. "At least you know who to tattle to." He tried for a joke.

Her lips tilted, but she was still...not sold on him; whether she didn't believe he was serious or wasn't interested in his proposal, he wasn't sure.

"Do you like living here?" he finally asked. How could he explain how he'd come to the rationalization that a marriage of convenience was a good idea? He could hardly say, *my dad thought this was a good idea*. Yeah, he bet that would win her over.

It sounded even more crazy to say he thought it was God's will.

"I do. It's a beautiful house, although it does need some work, and Joel said," she gave a little smile like she felt bad bringing up his friend's name and rubbing in that she did have permission, "that I could make any changes I wanted to. He said he trusted me, and he was sure you wouldn't mind. So I did replace the stairs on the back porch, and I painted the upstairs hall after I fixed the holes in the plaster."

Her eyes went around the kitchen. "I did a few little cosmetic updates here too. I guess I told you I didn't have a lot of money, but I didn't have a lot of time either because we were pretty busy this fall. I had some more things I was thinking about doing this winter. Just in case you didn't come back." She smiled. Maybe to let him know that it wasn't that she didn't want him there.

"If you marry me, you can make all the changes you want. This winter and any other time." Wow. Was that all he could think of to offer to convince her to take a chance on him? *You can make changes to the house.* Boy. There should be a school for someone as romantically challenged as he was.

She looked down at her hands, studying them like they would give her advice if she just waited long enough.

"I don't want to push you into something you definitely don't want. I mean, I can see why you might not want to marry me. We don't exactly know each other. But your kids need a dad, and although I am not familiar with kids and don't really know that much about them, I can try to be a good dad. And a good husband. And I'm more than capable of providing for you. It would ease your burden of worry and give you someone to share the load with."

He couldn't really think of anything else to use to sell himself.

She hadn't looked up through his whole speech, short as it was. He wished he'd written something down. Maybe he could have made himself sound a little better if he'd spent the night figuring out his good qualities and writing them down.

The seconds ticked by, and he let them. Maybe she just needed to think.

Her shoulders went up, almost like she was taking a deep breath to fortify herself, and his stomach churned. He'd have his answer in the next five seconds.

He held his breath.

She looked up, her eyes meeting his, a little scared but determined. "I'm sorry, but no. Your offer is too kind. So much kinder than what I deserve. But no. I made a decision a few months ago where I almost made a huge mistake, and of course I've made many more mistakes before then and since then. And I'm just not going to go there. I'm not going to take what seems to be the easy way out." She looked back at her hands and thought for a second before she glanced up again. "I'm just going to trust the Lord, and I'm going to let him work this out for me. Where we're going to go, what we're going to do, how we're going to survive."

"Did it ever occur to you that maybe this *is* the Lord opening a door? Maybe *this* is the door you're supposed to step through?"

Her eyes went sideways, and she swallowed. "Maybe. But the answer is still no. Thank you for offering."

Well, this was a little awkward. His first marriage proposal in his life, and he got a flat no.

Somehow, he thought getting down on his knee wouldn't help.

He was saved from having to say anything more when there was a knock at the door. He hadn't even heard anyone pull in. He'd been so focused on their conversation.

Natalie started to push up, then she looked at him, questions in her eyes. It was his house.

"Go ahead. It's probably for you anyway." He shrugged.

She pushed back, and he stood too, figuring he'd go out and take a walk.

He kind of felt like he let his dad down. He'd tried to get her to marry him, did the best he could at convincing her, and it wasn't enough.

A familiar voice echoed in through the mudroom, and a few seconds later, his mom appeared.

"Looks like this visitor was for you." Natalie smiled with true affection at his mother.

"I love my son, and I've barely seen him in months, so I definitely want more time with him, but I'm actually here to see you, Natalie."

"Me?" Natalie said, like she just couldn't believe someone would be there to talk to her.

"Yes. You. And," she lowered her eyes at Denver, "there are three cars out there, near the stand. I believe they are people looking for Christmas trees. This is usually a very busy day for people buying trees. You might want to go out and see what you can do for them."

"Oh my goodness. There are people here?" Natalie ran to the window and pulled back the curtain.

He suppressed a grin at her childlike enthusiasm.

Oddly, another thing that went through his mind was whether those curtains had been there or whether she put them up. They were lacy and cute and gave a soft, feminine touch to the kitchen.

He guessed they were from Natalie. And he liked the whimsical way they suited the way she was acting.

"Oh my goodness. There are people here! They're actually here! Wow!" She turned around, her cheeks red, her eyes sparkling. "I wasn't sure whether anyone would come. I mean, I didn't do any advertising." Her eyes shifted to Denver. "For you. I didn't do any advertising for you." It was like she was correcting herself and had been allowing herself to think this was hers.

And yet, she just turned him down. Why?

"I'll go take care of them. I've never sold Christmas trees, so this might be my first." He started toward the door but then turned back around. "What are we charging for them?"

"I don't know! Can you look up online and see what Christmas trees are going for?"

He pulled the phone out of his pocket. "I can do that."

"Thank you," she said, almost shyly, as he turned back around. He'd almost disappeared in the mudroom before she called after him, "Denver?"

He stopped. Was she going to change her mind about his proposal?

"There are handsaws in the shed behind the market. I think they must be for cutting Christmas trees down."

"Thanks."

Guess not.

He didn't know her, wasn't sure how much he liked her, so he had no idea why he was so disappointed.

Chapter Twelve

Natalie put her hand over her stomach as Denver walked out the door. She couldn't believe she turned him down. Why?

Well, she knew why. After she sent that crazy email to Welder Man, she determined she would never do another marriage of convenience, never even think about another marriage of convenience. It had been a foolish idea, one that had not been showing faith but a lack of it. She wasn't going to make that mistake again.

After she'd made the same mistake—over and over again—with men and trusting the wrong guy, she'd finally wised up.

Thankfully, it hadn't taken as long to get smart about thinking a marriage of convenience would solve all her problems.

She turned toward Mrs. Steiner. "Can I get you some tea?"

Thankfully, her children were still in the playroom and still quiet. That did not necessarily mean anything good. Quietness.

Sometimes it meant that they were busy getting into trouble. Hopefully no one got hurt until she was done entertaining Mrs. Steiner.

It was nice to have a woman to talk to. And Mrs. Steiner had come several times over the fall months when she'd been selling and picking apples and given her a hand.

"No, thank you. I'm not planning on staying long. But if you don't mind, I'd like to sit down."

"Of course. Please." She took the glass that Denver hadn't touched and set it in the sink. He was such a strong man. Steady, unruffled. He oozed confidence and capableness, like he could do anything.

They probably would make a good team. She would definitely love having a man like that around, anyway. Someone to take some of the burden off her, and once they weren't so nervous, he seemed to have a sense of humor. That would be nice too.

Trouble was she couldn't figure out what was in it for him.

Mrs. Steiner sat down on the long end of the table, so Natalie went around and sat directly across from her.

"It's good to see you. I hope nothing's wrong," she said, dying to know what would make Mrs. Steiner come for a casual visit.

"I don't want to take up too much of your time. I have a feeling you're going to get very busy today, and it's only," she looked at her watch, "11 o'clock."

"I hope so." She truly did.

Maybe, since Denver was home, she wouldn't get any of the money from the Christmas trees. But she hardly even cared; she was just excited about selling them. Too bad no one had shaped them this summer. She'd done some research on it and knew that they needed to be shaped with hedge trimmers in order to really look like real Christmas trees.

It wasn't too late. Maybe if she had time, she could put her focus on that.

If she found hedge trimmers lying around. She'd have to look. Actually, she had to figure out what they were before she went looking for them. She had no idea what hedge trimmers looked like.

"My husband and I have been talking about you," Mrs. Steiner began.

"Good things, I hope?" she said, hating the insecure note that crept into her voice.

"Of course. You're such a good mom. You're so responsible. And you're such a hard worker. Honestly, we've been admiring you. Taking this place, and instead of just squatting here, for lack of a better word, you made it better." She waved her arm around the room. "Look at the curtains. And the other improvements you've made. Plus, everyone talked about being able to go and get apples here despite the fact that Mr. Ziglar had sold. We were all afraid the apple orchard that made Mistletoe special and that drew people in would be closed down. You kept it up."

"The kids and I had fun." That was one hundred percent true, too. Natalie had loved every second of picking apples and selling them and making cider and having her kids involved.

"That was a lot of work," Mrs. Steiner said wisely.

"It was."

"I worried about you. Five kids is a lot of work. More than enough for one person...it's supposed to be two." She put her hand on the table as though to ward off any arguments. "I'm not saying anything bad about you. I think it's good you left your husband if he was abusive. Absolutely. I don't think anyone would argue with that. But what I am saying is being a mom is hard. Having five kids is hard. It was meant to be done by two people."

"You're right. It is hard. And the kids do need a dad." Did Mrs. Steiner know that Denver had been going to propose?

"My husband spoke with Denver last night after we had Thanksgiving dinner. He was convinced that Denver would make a perfect husband for you."

Now everything made sense. Pastor Race had told Denver to ask her to marry him.

Wait! What? Pastor Race had suggested a marriage of convenience?

That's crazy. Normal people didn't do that.

"Pastor Race?" she finally squeaked out.

"I know. I was shocked too. We've never even considered anything like this before. If someone needs help, the church helps them. And that's why I'm here." She patted Natalie's hand, her fingers warm and smooth. "We have that big old house, and all those kids that used to fill it up with so much fun and noise and laughter and busyness are pretty much all gone. Journee and Blakely are still around, and West comes in and out. But...we've got a lot of bedrooms, and I'd love to have you."

Natalie couldn't help it; her eyelids fluttered up and down. Finally, she got her eyes under control and stared at the wrinkled hand on top of hers. Considering. "You mean Pastor Race thinks Denver should marry me, and you want me to say no and move into your house?"

Mrs. Steiner chuckled. "No. I actually think that Race is right about this. However, I can imagine that must be quite a shock to you. As far as I know, you've never even met Denver before, other than church, where you probably didn't talk to him." She said it like it was kind of a statement but ended on a high note like she was asking a question, and Natalie shook her head.

"I talked to him a little when he came to see Ethan. That was the first I'd ever spoken to him. It was basically 'hi, how are you.' Nothing more."

"That's what I thought. And although I agree with Pastor Race that the idea is perfect, I didn't think he'd understand maybe the way a woman feels." Mrs. Steiner smiled in such a warm and nurturing way that it almost made Natalie want to go over and sit on her lap, to be a little girl again and have a mom who actually held her and put her arms around her and told her that everything was going to be okay. Or even if she didn't tell her that everything was going to be okay, who at least told her that she could do it. And that her mom would be beside her, holding her hand, cheering her on.

She wanted that so bad it was like an ache in her chest.

"Thank you. I appreciate the consideration." Even if it wasn't necessary.

Funny, that was the thing that Mrs. Steiner chose to be concerned about.

Wouldn't she be shocked if she had known that Natalie had sent an email to a random stranger asking him to marry her and ended up sending it to the wrong random stranger? She'd been completely willing to marry anyone who wasn't going to hurt her children.

Sight unseen.

Guilt made the bridge of her nose feel tight, and she had to say, "Your concern makes me feel loved in a way that I've never felt before. But...that's really not the problem. I guess I'd marry anyone, figuring that as long as he didn't hit me and as long as he was kind to my kids, I could handle it. But I was at that point after camp was over and they were going to sell—and then condemned—my house. But there were a bunch of different things that happened, and I realized that I wasn't allowing the Lord to work in my life the way He wanted to. I was rushing ahead and doing things my own way. And I didn't want to continue to do that."

Mrs. Steiner was nodding sagely, and Natalie felt like she had a great point. "I understand. I've done that. I left my first marriage when I shouldn't have. But we're not talking about my mistakes." She gave a gentle smile. "I made a lot of them."

Natalie smiled back.

"Maybe, this is God opening a door for you. Consider that." She lifted a shoulder.

Funny how Denver had just said the same thing. It was almost uncanny.

Mrs. Steiner continued. "If marrying Denver even though you don't know him very well doesn't concern you, it could be that this is what the Lord wants. Race seems sure of it. And," she patted her hand again, "I can personally vouch for Denver. You couldn't get a better man."

Natalie had to agree with that. Although part of her head said that Welder Man was a good man too.

There had never been anything but friendship between them though. Here she had a marriage proposal in front of her—unless it was rescinded when she turned him down.

"Everyone will think this is crazy."

"You can't live your life based on what everyone thinks. You also can't live your life based on the world's standards. Because God never talks about falling in love in the Bible. He talks about love, yes. But it's love as an action verb. Being patient, being kind, being gentle, being good, not being prideful, and putting others ahead of yourself. That's what love is. According to God. It's the world that puts these tingly hot feelings in it."

"So you don't believe in love?"

Mrs. Steiner shook her head. "I believe in the Bible's definition of love. And since we're commanded to do it, we can make those feelings come, or if they come for the wrong person, we can ignore them and make them go away. Because God wouldn't give us a command that we can't follow, right?"

That was kind of new. She had never considered that.

"Mom! Mom!" Jack came running in. "Mom! Do you see all the cars?"

Natalie had her mouth open to reprimand her son for coming in and interrupting their conversation without waiting to be acknowledged, but at his words, she jumped up from the table herself and ran over to the window. There were fifteen cars in the parking lot by the market.

"Oh my goodness. Do you think they're all here for Christmas trees?"

Mrs. Steiner had gotten up, somewhat slower and with more dignity, to come over and look as well.

"I bet they are. It is Black Friday, and I bet this is probably one of the biggest Christmas tree-buying days of the year."

"I wouldn't know. I've never bought a Christmas tree." She'd never had the money to spend on anything so frivolous.

If she stayed here, she would have a Christmas tree, and she wouldn't even have to pay for it.

She almost laughed.

Was she really at the point where she would consider marrying a man just because she'd have a Christmas tree? Goodness. She thought she was desperate before.

"If you don't mind, I think I need to get out there. I bet Denver's pretty overwhelmed." If he was trying to help people cut their Christmas trees down and take payment for them, he would be running in circles.

She thought there was a wrapper and a shaker somewhere…and they were so unprepared.

"Of course. This is your business. Go do it. I can see myself out." Mrs. Steiner patted her shoulder before waving her fingers and walking herself out the door.

Natalie took one more look out the window before she went to get her kids to take them outside and give Denver a hand.

Chapter Thirteen

*D*enver put the trunk of the tree in the vibrator that would shake the dead pine needles and other loose debris out of the tree before it was wrapped. There were three people standing in line waiting to check out at the market stand.

Normally they could just pay for their own, put their money in a can or something, but he'd been informed by the first customer that the way the previous owner had done it was they had to put a five-dollar deposit on their handsaw, then when they came back with their tree, they had their five-dollar deposit taken out of the cost of the tree when they turned in their saw.

Several people had said that they wanted to pick a tree up that was already cut and shook and wrapped.

They didn't have any of those.

So he'd been trying to take care of shaking and wrapping peoples' trees plus handle the saws and check people out.

He'd been doing pretty good at keeping up for the first thirty minutes, then things got crazy.

Thankfully, that was about the time Natalie stepped out of the house.

He loved the way she moved. There was a grace about her but also a bounce in her step; it just spoke of energy or excitement or fun or something. She was laughing at something that one of the kids said, and they all bounded around beside her, except the little one which she carried.

He wondered what in the world she was going to do to help with all those kids. It was a full-time job just watching them.

"How long does it have to do that?" the man in front of him asked. He and his wife, who were probably in their late twenties or early thirties, had two little kids who were practically jumping up and down with excitement, watching their tree get shaken.

Denver took a minute to enjoy their excitement and to savor the feeling of being the one to cause it.

"Not very long. It's been long enough," Denver said. Way more than long enough. He'd been too busy watching Natalie to pay any attention to the tree. He put it on the wrapper and turned it on.

The equipment had been easy to use and simple to learn. Because of his job, he was good at figuring stuff out, anyway.

He didn't recognize this couple, but he hadn't been in Mistletoe much the last 10 years or so. Then even before that, he'd been learning to weld and dive and not been around much.

There were probably a lot of people he wouldn't know or recognize.

"Are you going to have peaches next year?" the lady asked as the wrapper finished.

Denver looked around. Did he have peaches? Were there peaches on the farm?

Natalie had mentioned apples. He'd thought that was crazy, since he'd spent most of the fall studying apples. He couldn't wait to go see the trees—find out what varieties he had and whether they were a modern, intensive system or older dwarf or even standard trees.

He had intended to do that this afternoon after he got things settled with Natalie.

Three more cars formed a parade coming in his driveway, and he kinda had the feeling that maybe he wouldn't be going to look at apple trees.

If he had any spare time at all, he probably ought to spend it cutting Christmas trees down.

"These Christmas trees aren't shaped as nicely as they have been in past years. Did you guys not trim them this year?" asked a man standing in line waiting for his tree to be shaken and wrapped.

Did trees need to be trimmed? He had no clue.

Maybe he bit off more than he could chew with this farm thing.

No, he knew he could do it. He just hadn't been here.

"I'm not sure about either one of your questions. I just bought the farm, and I need to make a five-year plan, and then we'll go from there."

He hoped that sounded slightly intelligent. Did farms have five-year plans?

Natalie had reached the market, the kids had dispersed, and she was taking care of the customers that had been waiting to check out. Her kids ran around. The little one stood up in some kind of play yard thing that he hadn't seen earlier, so she must have just set it up. Maybe it had been in the market and he'd missed it.

The afternoon grew steadily busier as people seemed to return from their Black Friday Christmas shopping, deciding they wanted to grab a tree while they were at it.

His stomach was growling, and he was thirsty, as suppertime came and went.

He'd just finished wrapping a tree and had directed the man carrying it over to the market to pay Natalie when something tugged at his shirt.

"Hey, mister," a small voice beside him said.

He looked down at the little girl that had been bleeding in the bathroom. She had a Band-Aid over her forehead now, and he couldn't remember the name that Natalie had said. Ramona? Maybe. "Yeah?"

"Here." She held up a cold bottle of water and a sandwich with what might be turkey in it. He looked at her fingers; he'd seen sidewalks that were cleaner, but he was kinda hungry and he wasn't being picky.

"That was awfully nice of you. Miss Ramona?"

Her chin went up and down and up and down in a cute, jerky way.

"Thank you," he said as he took the sandwich from her hand. Only two pieces of turkey fell out from the bottom before he could squeeze it tight.

"Mommy made it."

"You can tell your mom I appreciate it."

Her little brows tilted in, and her eyes clinched up. "'Preciate?"

"Tell her I said 'thank you.' Tell her…" He wasn't sure if the little girl could deliver the message or not, but he figured he'd try. "Thanks for thinking of me."

The little girl nodded again and skipped off.

He noticed then that the other four children were sitting at the picnic table, with the oldest one feeding the youngest one what looked like maybe Cheerios, and the rest of them had sandwiches.

Natalie was checking customers out again; if she'd eaten a sandwich, he hadn't seen it.

"I'll put your tree on the shaker, and then I'll be right back," he said to the man who was next. The fellow, in overalls with a big gray beard, nodded and looked at his wife, who looked exactly like him except no beard.

"You eat your sandwich, sonny. We been standing here for a while. Won't hurt us none to stand here for another five minutes. You get some supper in your gizzard." The lady's green eyes sparkled, set as they were in a face wreathed with laugh lines. She looked about as friendly as everyone else who had been here today.

Man, he hadn't spent nearly enough time in his hometown. He needed to fix that.

Sticking his sandwich in his mouth and holding it there while he uncapped his bottle of water, he grabbed a hold of it again, chugging half the bottle before taking a bite of sandwich and walking over.

Chewing was overrated. That's what his parents had always teased him that he thought, anyway, and the sandwich was in his stomach before he made it to the market. The bottled water was empty.

"Did you eat?" he asked when he was just a couple of feet away from Natalie's side.

She had just taken a handsaw from a customer and given him a total for his tree, and she jerked her head around. She hadn't known he was coming.

"I will. I'm just busy."

"Go sit down and eat. You haven't eaten anything all day." If she'd had any lunch, he missed it. Maybe she ate breakfast. But he wasn't going to quibble over the details.

Her eyes flashed. He figured she didn't appreciate being told what to do.

"Are you stopping to eat too?"

"My sandwich is already in my stomach. I'd show you, but it might gross someone out."

She pursed her lips. He figured he'd probably been on a ship surrounded by men for way too long, because she didn't really think his humor was very funny.

Okay. He needed to try to do a little better.

He thought he'd be relieved she told him no. He found, though, that he kind of wanted her, if not to accept his marriage proposal, to at least like him.

He definitely seemed to like watching her anyway. He liked the way her eyes flashed. He definitely liked the fact that she thought of him when she was feeding everyone.

Someone needed to think of her.

He was as good as anyone for that job.

"Go eat. I'll check these people out."

"You have people waiting on you. You also have a tree on the shaker."

"They said they'd wait five minutes. You've got five minutes to eat. You're wasting it."

Her eyes cut to the people waiting, and then they went back to him. Her lips pressed closed, and he supposed, if they had any conversation later at all, he was going to hear about giving her orders.

She was probably right about that too. Another drawback from being the man in charge on a ship full of men.

Not the captain, just the job boss.

So, maybe he needed to develop a few different techniques for dealing with Natalie. Something a little softer. A little gentler.

And not the way he dealt with his sisters. Because he probably would have told them to stick their finger in his mouth and touch the back of his throat, and he would show them what he ate.

Probably not the best way to convince someone to marry him.

He ended up checking out three people before Natalie came back.

"I ate."

"Thank you." He stepped away from the counter as the next person stepped up.

She waited until he was beside her, and then, almost grudgingly, she looked over at him. "Thank you."

"It was kind of you to think of me along with your kids and yourself. I wasn't really expecting it. I was pretty hungry and dry. Thanks."

She nodded, almost embarrassed by his gratefulness and by his show of appreciation.

He went on over and took the tree out of the shaker, chatting with the folks and working some more.

It'd just been a sandwich and a bottle of water, but it was kindness that was unexpected, and yeah, she'd been living in his house without rent, but he didn't think that was why she'd given him the sandwich and the water.

If anything, he might expect her to be upset that she was having to move out.

Except she didn't have to.

It'd been getting darker, and he looked around and realized that there were some bright lights on the light poles down by the parking lot. But while there was a light pole near where he was, the lights on it weren't working.

He thought when he'd gone to look for the saws that he'd seen boxes that looked like they had light bulbs in them. Maybe they might be the right ones.

Maybe there was a ladder to use to change them in there too. If not...he gave the pole a once-over. He could climb that.

He'd goofed around with sailors many times before, and he had a few tricks he could use. Actually, it'd be easier without the up-and-down motion of the ship.

He wrapped one more tree and then said, "If you guys would hold on for a second, so I can change the light bulbs up here on this light pole, I'd appreciate it."

There were three people in line, and two of them seemed okay with it.

The lady in the back with two small children bouncing around her didn't look real happy, but her husband seemed okay, if not a little resigned. So Denver walked back over toward the market to the shed that was beside it.

This wasn't nearly as exciting as his normal job, but there was something fun about providing a service to his neighbors. Providing Christmas trees. Something that would decorate their home and cover their gifts and be a central piece of their season. It was a nice thought.

Grabbing the things he needed, he looked over at the woman behind the counter. It was also nice to have someone working with him.

Chapter Fourteen

atalie glanced around while she waited for the next customer to come to the counter.

Denver wasn't at the shaker machine anymore. Where had he gone?

Kole had been fussy, so she held him on one hip and bounced him slowly.

Thankfully she'd just changed his diaper, and his head was drooping to her shoulder. If they were at the house, she'd be putting him to bed.

He'd started out more than a few nights this fall in his pack and play when they were picking apples in the orchard, so she knew he'd be okay.

As she was considering, Denver came out of the shed with some kind of wide strap and a little bag over his shoulder.

She greeted the next lady in line and accepted her five dollars as she reached for a saw, all the while keeping her eye on Denver.

He was walking to the light pole.

"Hey, Natalie. Looks like Denver's back in town. How'd you get him to help you here?"

Natalie took her eyes off the broad shoulders that had stopped in front of the light pole. Denver was doing something with the strap he held in his hand. She wanted to watch, but she turned toward the voice.

Dakota Whitney. She had two elementary school-age children and commuted to what Natalie understood to be a prestigious job in Cedar Heights, a resort town an hour north.

"I guess he just wanted to," Natalie said, not wanting to get into the fact that Denver actually owned the farm. It wasn't a widely known fact, since he'd basically bought it using Joel. She wasn't even sure he'd actually seen the whole farm.

He hadn't gotten a chance to do that today, either.

"If he's looking for something to do, he can come over and help me. I've got plenty of things to do at my house." Dakota's voice seemed to purr as she reached for the handsaw that Natalie held out.

"I suppose you could ask him," Natalie said, feeling kinda subdued.

Dakota obviously wouldn't mind having Denver. If Denver had offered Dakota a marriage of convenience, she would take him up on it.

Natalie didn't believe in bowing to peer pressure. She couldn't help but think it influenced her to think that someone else probably thought she was nuts for saying no today.

"Last year, there were trees that were already cut that we could buy," Dakota said, her nails sparkling in the overhead light as she gingerly took the handsaw from Natalie.

"This year, there's not. Not today anyway. Maybe tomorrow, if you want to wait." Natalie raised her brows and held onto the saw while Dakota pursed her lips.

"Maybe once Denver is done changing that light, he'll come back and cut a tree down for me. Is he just hanging out here, or are you paying him?"

Usually small towns were hotbeds for gossip, but Denver's family didn't seem like the type to spread things, and Natalie guessed that not too many people knew the truth about what was going on with the farm.

They probably wondered though. People had assumed she was renting it and running it herself. Which was nuts.

If the previous owner hadn't sprayed the apples and taken care of them, she wouldn't have had an apple crop.

She had no idea of how to do that herself.

She wasn't sure she wanted to learn. It seemed kind of complicated.

The Christmas trees, though, she could have shaped them if she'd had time.

It was hard to do things with the kids. The older kids rode their bikes in the parking lot while Sky cuddled up with her blanket on a beanbag in the back corner.

Natalie looked over her shoulder. Yeah, her thumb was in her mouth, and she was sound asleep.

"Natalie, are you going to answer me?" Dakota said.

"I don't know."

"You don't know if you're paying him?"

"I'm not paying him."

Dakota sighed, put out. "So he's just hanging out here?"

Natalie looked over again. He was actually climbing the light pole.

Her stomach twisted. "I guess."

"Well then, he's fair game." Dakota took her saw. "I sure hope he stays around a little longer this time. Someone will get lucky with him." She winked at Natalie. "And I hope that lucky girl is me." She looked around. "Come on, boys. Let's go."

Denver had made it to the top of the light pole. He unscrewed the bulb after removing the covering.

All he used to stay up on the pole was the rope that went around the back of his waist and also around the pole. He leaned back against it, keeping the tension tight.

Natalie had to admit her heart was in her throat.

What was he thinking?

He was high enough up that if anything were to happen, he would fall. If he didn't die, he'd be lucky.

The guy was crazy.

The light blinked on, illuminating the area down where he had been working and where people milled about with their trees.

The new cars coming down the lane had slowed to a trickle, so surely things would be clearing out soon, but they still needed the light.

He adjusted the small bag on his back and somehow moved himself in a circle around the pole to change the other light that was also burnt out.

Natalie thought about the past summer and how she'd worked like crazy from the time she got up in the morning until she fell into bed at night. Having Denver around would have been really nice.

A team effort rather than a solo job. That was always more fun.

Denver was a little bossy; he tried to boss her around earlier, but she bet he'd be a good person to work with. Obviously, he saw things that needed to be done and did them.

She could admire a take-charge, get-things-done kind of personality. And she supposed, as long as he knew that she reserved the right to refuse, she was okay if he didn't say things in a pretty way, asking properly instead of commanding.

She could get on board with doing what he wanted.

What was she thinking?

She was going to start looking for rentals tomorrow morning. She and Denver weren't going to be working together on anything.

Maybe she'd been a little hasty in her decision.

Maybe this really was the Lord opening a door.

How could she tell?

It definitely wasn't something she'd sought out, trying to rush ahead. Maybe that was the difference. She'd been waiting, working while she was waiting, and this door opened.

Maybe that was it. Work and be prepared.

Denver had finished with the other light, and it was on. As she watched, he fitted the cover over the top of it and started down the pole, loosening the tension as he went down.

The two people standing in line were watching, so Natalie turned her attention back to Denver as he made it to the ground.

Dakota stood there waiting for him. She rushed over, putting her hand on his arm and talking to him.

Natalie looked back at the customer in front of her. "May I help you?"

After that, she spent a good hour waiting on people before Denver came over.

This time, she saw him, because goodness help her, she'd been keeping an eye on him.

He wasn't always wrapping trees. He'd gone and cut some down for people. One of those people had been Dakota, Natalie couldn't help but notice.

"Do we have more rope for the wrapper?" Denver asked when she met his eyes.

"I believe so," she said, scrunching her brows up, trying to think where she'd seen the spools of rope and wondered what they were for. "Excuse me for a moment," she said to the person standing at the counter. "I think they're back here. There was a stack of them…" She walked back and pointed to the spool.

Denver stopped, looking at it. "Thanks," he said, his eyes moving back to her. "I want you to take the kids in and get them to bed. I can handle things since they've slowed down. There's no one coming to rent saws anymore, and that takes a lot of time."

This was a little different than before when he'd given her a command to go in. To eat.

She narrowed her eyes at him. "I can work a little longer."

"Might be better for the kids to go to bed." His voice didn't hold any censor, and she didn't feel judged, but she did feel a little pushed.

Her feet ached, her back was tired, and she still had a lot of work ahead of her to scrub the kids up and get them in bed.

"I don't want to lose any business because people say they have to wait a long time to be waited on here."

"If we lose a couple customers because you and the kids go inside and get the rest you need, it's okay."

She sighed, not wanting to give in.

"Go on," he urged. "I've got it."

"Okay. I'll do what you want."

He touched her arm, and her eyes flew to his. That odd stirring that she had any time she was close to him intensified with his hand, just his fingers really, on her arm.

"Think maybe someone needs to take care of you. Because you seem to be taking care of everyone else."

His words caused her throat to close.

How many times had she wished that there was someone, not necessarily to take care of her but to help her?

So many times.

Mrs. Steiner had said it was too much for one person to do by themselves. Raising kids wasn't something one person was supposed to do alone.

"I guess I've survived this long. I'll probably just keep surviving." It wasn't a very good answer, but it was the best she could come up with. She moved away from his hand, and it dropped.

They slid by each other, the smell of hazelnut mixing with that scent she'd noticed from before, strong and sure with confidence and laughter. She didn't know a scent could remind her of so much. There was a draw there too.

Maybe, she'd wait up after she put the kids in bed and see if his offer was still open.

She hadn't declined him because of Welder Man.

But there was a pinch in her heart, not her heart exactly but just the idea that she had thought that maybe there could be more sometime between them. But she had a real live man, a good man, in front of her now.

Maybe that open door really was from the Lord.

Chapter Fifteen

*D*enver walked slowly up the steps and into the mudroom, carrying a money bag with everything that had been in the cash register.

He'd had no idea when he'd bought this farm that it had a thriving Christmas tree operation.

It had been nonstop work since they stepped out shortly before lunch. But he was pretty sure they'd made a lot of money.

He didn't really have to make anything since he'd been saving up most of his salary, but it was nice to know he'd stepped into a profitable operation.

He opened the door, and the smell of Thanksgiving hit him.

Natalie stood with her back to him at the stove, stirring something. Maybe gravy?

Her hair hung down her back, dark and curly. She had on a floor-length skirt and a long-sleeved T-shirt. He thought he saw a toe sticking out, so he was guessing her feet were bare.

It didn't matter; the kitchen smelled heavenly.

"Sorry I'm so late." He hadn't expected her to wait up for him. Hadn't considered that she might.

"I thought I saw the last car leave fifteen or twenty minutes ago, and I figured you'd be in. I assume you're hungry?" She turned around with her question in her eyes.

"I am. That smells really good."

"Leftovers from yesterday. I hope that's okay."

"It's perfect."

After spending the last part of the summer and all fall on a ship with no cook, anything that didn't have tuna in it would be good.

He got himself a glass and filled it with tea, loving that she had it ready in the refrigerator. By the time he had gotten a plate and silverware out, she had the pans on the table. She seemed to bustle around a little, like she was nervous. Did he make her nervous?

He set the money bag down. "I didn't count that, but we sold a lot of trees today. There's a good bit there."

She nodded. "I was shocked. I had no idea there would be that many people. I wonder if today is usually the busiest day?"

He shrugged. "I don't know. I would think it would get busier as Christmas gets closer, but I don't know."

He sat down, and she arranged the pots so he could serve himself.

"You didn't need to wait up."

"I know. I wanted to."

He'd been spooning mashed potatoes on his plate, but her comment made him look at her, really look at her. She looked serious, and she was biting her lip. Odd.

"I appreciate what you did tonight. It can't be easy working with all those kids. If they'll go with me, I could take a couple." He paused without meaning to. "If you're gonna be here tomorrow."

He tried to keep his voice unemotional like he wasn't hoping that she would be, even though he was. Maybe he should let her know. It just seemed like it would be easier for him, and less awkward for both of them, if he didn't beg her to stay when she was determined to leave.

Plus, if the Lord wanted it to work out, it wasn't really up to him to change her mind.

"If you don't mind, I was going to stay and help."

"I don't mind. I appreciate it." He scooped gravy over the top of the stuffing balls and potatoes and turkey that he'd put on his plate.

She pulled a chair out and sat down. He noticed that she didn't sit at the other end of the table from him but actually pulled out the chair on his right and sat there. He wasn't sure what that meant, if anything.

"I have a couple of ideas of things that can make tomorrow go smoother," she began, almost hesitantly.

"Me too. I wasn't expecting today to be so crazy. What are your ideas?"

"Well, Maggie and Jack can be in charge of renting out the handsaws. And they can do that in a separate line. I didn't take the time to teach them today, because I hadn't been expecting it at first, and then I wasn't sure what you would think. They're not that old. Only seven and eight."

He nodded, his mouth full. He wasn't really thinking about handsaws though or Christmas trees. He was looking at her thinking if her oldest child was eight that meant she would have to be...at least twenty-six, twenty-seven, maybe even thirty.

She had some fine lines on her face, but he thought they were more from exhaustion than age.

He wouldn't have guessed her to be a day over twenty-five.

He didn't know that much about women, though.

He swallowed, holding his spoon in the air. "That sounds like a good idea. They should be able to handle that. It's not hard. Unless they have to make change, and in that case..."

"Maggie's actually really good at math. And Jack is really good at talking to people. I thought they would make a good team and be able to handle it."

He nodded. "I'll take your word for it. You know your kids better than I do."

If there was going to be a marriage of convenience, he needed to get to know her kids.

So he said, "I don't know the little guy's name, but I can hold him. He can go around with me for the most part."

"I don't want him to get in your way."

"I wouldn't have offered if he was gonna be in my way."

"Well, he'll need his diaper changed and all that."

"I know where you are." He grinned. Okay, if there was a marriage of convenience, he might have to learn how to change diapers, but there was no need to rush anything.

At his words, she looked up from where she was studying her hands or the condensation on the glass of tea and smiled at him. "Spoken like a man."

"That's what I am."

She almost laughed. He was sure of it.

"I also was thinking tomorrow morning I can get up early and go cut some trees down, shake them, and wrap them. I think that'll make things go a lot easier if I'm not trying to cut trees down as well as help people shake and wrap."

"That's a brilliant idea. I never got any of the trees shaped this fall. I was too busy doing other things."

"Yeah, I saw some of them were a little scraggly."

"I've never done it before, but it can't be that hard. Maybe I can work on doing that?"

"That's fine with me. I figure if we started at daylight, which is around seven-ish, maybe seven-thirty-ish maybe, we can get in at least four hours of work before the first customers arrive."

"I don't know how many trees I can get shaped in that amount of time, but it would be worth a try."

"That's what I thought. If you're not eating, you can count the money in there." He jerked his head at the money bag.

"That's yours."

"Ours. You were there too."

"You own the farm."

"And I'm splitting it with you. You going to count? Or are you going to sit there and argue with me?" He grinned to take away any sting that might have been in his words. He liked that she didn't make assumptions, although he wouldn't mind it if she had.

There were some checks, and she set those aside. Most people had paid in cash.

"If we're going to keep doing this, we should get set up so we can take credit cards."

She answered without looking up. "That's a really good idea. People like to pay with cards. Although, I think when they come here, they know we can't take them, so I didn't have too much problem with people thinking that they were going to and having to turn them away."

"That's good to hear. I don't know if we can do that this year or not." He paused, his eyes on her. "That's making the assumption that you're going to be here through the season."

He said that slowly, carefully, like he was feeling his way. He didn't want to push her, didn't want to scare her, and didn't want her to know that for some reason, he really wanted her to stay.

She spun the glass in her fingers, slowly, looking at the wet mark it made on the table. Finally, she pursed her lips and looked up. "I wanted to talk to you about that."

His eyes shot to her. "About what?" A softness, a feeling of lightness gathered in his chest. It felt like...hope.

"About your offer."

"The one you turned down?" he couldn't help saying with a lifted lip.

There was something compelling about her, something strangely familiar even though he was sure he'd never met her before in his life, other than saying hi to her at his brother's house earlier that summer.

It just felt like he knew her. Like he was comfortable and familiar with her.

And he liked her.

She almost reminded him exactly of the way he'd pictured Mom of Five. Everything.

Only, this woman was the one that God had physically placed in his life. It seemed kind of crazy to walk away without fighting to keep her.

"I originally turned you down, yes. But I changed my mind. If the offer is still open?" She put her finger in the water ring and moved it slowly back and forth.

"It is." He didn't even hesitate. He wasn't playing a game like that.

She looked up then, her gaze steady. "Thank you. Thank you for making the offer. Thank you for not holding it against me that I turned it down without thinking about it."

"Decided I was a catch after all?" He grinned.

"Something like that." Maybe there was a little flirt in her voice. There was definitely a smile on her lips, and he liked that. It erased the years from her face and made her look almost like a teenager.

Which was impossible. She had five children.

"Are you sure?" he asked, setting his spoon down on his empty plate and pushing back from the table just a bit. "You can have time to think about it. You don't have to make a decision today."

"That's actually what your mom wanted to talk to me about."

A little thread of panic went through him. Had his mom told her that his dad had come up with the idea?

He wasn't great with women or anything, but he could only imagine that would insult her. Make her hate him even. The idea that he was proposing marriage because his dad wanted him to.

No matter how true it was, that couldn't be exactly what a woman wanted to hear—*I don't want you for yourself; I just want you because my dad said I should. You're a charity case.* Basically.

But that couldn't be, since his mom had managed to talk her into it.

"What did she say?" he finally managed to get out in what sounded like a normal tone to him.

"She said your dad suggested that it was a good idea." Her eyes were steady on his, and he tried not to flinch. She didn't seem upset, but put out in the open air like that between them, it most definitely seemed calloused and uncaring.

It's not what she deserved anyway.

"That's true." He couldn't deny it. He wouldn't.

As much as he'd like to say that there was something else, as much as he'd like to lie and spare her feelings, it wasn't right. So he wouldn't.

"But she said that she thought that that might be too much, too hard, to be married to someone one barely knew, that *I* barely knew, and she offered to allow the children and me to move into her home."

That took him aback.

Whose side was his mom on anyway? Sounded like she was against both his dad and him? Unless she assumed that he hadn't wanted to marry Natalie, and she was trying to help them out. Boy, he hoped she didn't come off like that.

No, his mom would never come off like that.

He hoped.

"It's an odd way to talk you into accepting my proposal," he finally said.

"Well, she said even though your dad was sure that it was the right thing to do, and she agreed with him, she thought that it might not be something that I would want. She wanted to make sure I had another option. That the church was taking care of me." She lifted her shoulder and tilted her head, kind of a I'm-not-sure-why shrug.

"But it was her saying all of that, and me knowing that you're a good man, and I would be blessed to have you. And my children even more so. I hope I'm not being selfish." Her eyes had dropped, but they looked back up at that last sentence, and he could see that she was sincere.

Obviously, after her children, her main concern was that she wasn't doing something that was going to cause regret for him.

"I'm thirty-three. It's not old, but it's old enough that I've been around. I know what I'm doing."

He wouldn't regret it at all. If he hadn't "met" Mom of Five, he wouldn't even have a shadow of a doubt in his head.

But that's not who God had in front of him right now, and as much as he liked her as a friend and had been interested in getting to know her more, Natalie was the one that God had put in his life. He wasn't going to turn the Lord down, and he definitely wasn't going to let his earthly father down.

"Okay then. I guess... I guess it's settled?"

He nodded. "Now we just need to find time. Tomorrow's Saturday, so we can't get a license tomorrow. Plus, it could be a busy day at that."

"I haven't been open on Sundays."

"I think that's what people expect then. We'll plan on that. How do you feel about getting a tree of our own and decorating it Sunday afternoon?"

Her eyes brightened, like she'd never gotten a Christmas tree before. Or like he'd offered her a diamond ring. Which, thinking about it, he'd proposed to her and offered her nothing.

Maybe she wasn't used to anything and wasn't disappointed. But that was no excuse to not do right by her.

He made a mental note to look at rings. Or at least ask about them, since he'd never bought a ring in his life before.

"I'd love that. That sounds like so much fun! I know the children will think it's the best thing ever."

He almost thought she was going to come across the table and hug him.

He was ready.

She didn't, and he laughed a little to himself. That was moving a little bit too fast probably. Considering they'd just really met for the first time today.

He still had some things he needed to tell her. That she needed to know.

"I'll be here for a week, but then I have to leave to go to a job. It should only last a week; it's the last one of the season. I've already promised, and I can't go back on my word."

He didn't want to explain to her about taking Crew's place and about Crew and all the things that happened over the summer.

They seemed so far away, like another world. It always did when he was off the ship.

He liked falling into this busy, productive, feeling-like-he-was-needed routine.

Loved the idea of growing something that people needed and wanted and would pay for, loved the idea of being on the farm and slowing down.

His eyes slid to Natalie. He loved the idea of being a husband and father too. He'd never been against it, but it was growing on him in a very good way.

"Okay. So you're leaving...when?"

"Next Friday afternoon. I have a buddy, Jonathan, who lives in Missouri. He'll be coming down through here. I can have him pick me up, and I can leave my pickup here. Just in case you need it for anything."

Her eyes opened and shut twice, and her brows lifted.

"Oh. Thank you. I appreciate that." She kind of looked like she wasn't sure what she would use it for, but the idea that he would leave his pickup there, for her, just like that, seemed to impress her.

If they were going to be married, why not?

Maybe she thought he was going to make her earn her place?

That wasn't the way he was thinking about it at all. He was thinking that his place was hers, just by virtue of becoming his wife.

He wasn't sure which of them was thinking wrong. Maybe there was no protocol for a marriage of convenience.

He didn't want to continue as a marriage of convenience though. He realized, almost without thinking about it, that he really wanted his wife to fall in love with him.

Chapter Sixteen

*S*unday morning, it was weird to come downstairs and have a man at her table.

Her kids found it odd as well. They were very quiet. Normally they couldn't eat without everyone chattering and talking and the occasional argument. But their eyes were wide and silent as they stared at the tall man as he stood at the stove and cooked sausage.

Saturday had been a blur of activity, and Natalie hadn't told the kids what Denver and she had decided the night before. She hadn't found the words this morning, either, when she got them up to get ready for breakfast and church.

How could she tell her kids it was like that? Maybe if he'd been around for a while, it would be a little different, but they didn't even know him, and she was going to marry him.

She had no concept of a marriage of convenience, knew no one who had done it, although surely other people had. But she just had no idea of how it should work.

Not to mention how it should work with her children.

Making sure that her kids were taken care of had always been her top priority.

Denver had a new-looking pair of jeans on and a plaid button-down shirt. She assumed that was what he was wearing to church.

Ramona was the first child to come down to the kitchen.

"Who's that?" she asked.

Ramona was one of those children who was wide-awake as soon as her eyes opened. She dragged at night, but she didn't miss a thing in the morning.

Natalie couldn't blame her for asking the question, but it was rude, so she corrected her, and then said, "This is Mr. Denver." As she spoke, she hesitated, her eyes lifting to Denver's.

They should have talked about what her kids were going to call him. Maybe he saw the questions on her face, because he smiled a little and shook his head. Like it didn't matter. It would work out. She liked that. No point in getting huffy about things.

Natalie had decided to make waffles, and as she measured the flour in the bowl, she heard Kole.

Putting the lid on the container, she slid it back and brushed her hands together.

"I can get him." Denver pushed the skillet to the back of the stove and turned the burner off.

Natalie looked at him. His eyes held questions, and she didn't know the answers to them.

Finally, she decided it wasn't going to hurt Kole at all to spend three minutes without his mother. "Okay. Thanks."

Their eyes held for just a bit more. What was he thinking? Did he regret his proposal? Would he eventually regret it?

Even for a couple that had been married for a long time, five kids was a lot.

Maybe that's why Welder Man and she had stayed just friends. Five kids was too much.

She wasn't going to think about him anymore. She'd committed to marrying someone else.

Jack and Maggie came in the kitchen together. Jack looked

behind him and said in a whisper, "Who's that man? He was here yesterday too. What's he doing here?"

"He's the owner of the house and farm."

Their eyes got big. Jack figured out what that meant just a few seconds before Maggie did.

"Does that mean we're going to have to move?" he asked in a small voice.

Sky hadn't gotten up yet, but she wouldn't be able to understand. So, Natalie looked at her three oldest kids, their big eyes looking back at her, and hoped that she wasn't making another major mistake in her life.

No. Denver most definitely wasn't a mistake.

"No. It doesn't. Mr. Denver, which is what you can call him, has agreed to marry me, and once we're married, we're staying here."

Talk about awkward. She could tell from the kids' expressions during her speech that this announcement was going to go over like lead bricks everywhere.

Church today might be an interesting experience to say the least. She hoped she was ready for it.

"Do you have any questions, children?" She felt like she was being excessively formal, but she didn't know how else to talk about it.

They all shook their heads. They were probably too young to have too many questions. Like, "What in the world were you thinking, Mom?"

She turned back to the counter and continued to mix the waffles.

She had the recipe memorized, thankfully, and was able to put it together quickly.

There was a waffle in the iron when Denver entered the doorway, Kole on one hip and Sky on the other.

Natalie's heart skipped about seventeen beats, and her hand went to her chest.

He looked so good holding her children.

He would be good to the kids; she was sure of that. He'd probably treat her okay too. And even if her heart longed for love, whatever that was, whatever form, she just...she didn't know. She just wanted to feel like she was important to someone.

Was that love?

Maybe love wasn't in God's plan for her. She didn't recall reading in the Bible anywhere where one had to love someone in order to get married.

God was providing a solution to all of her problems. What was the line about not looking a gift horse in the mouth?

She should be on her knees thanking him. Not worried about love, and not worried about what the rest of the world was thinking either.

She wasn't going to worry about any of that.

It probably didn't bode well for her that she didn't want to take her eyes off him. She might be a pity marriage for him, although he would probably deny it, but if she were in love with him, if she were to fall in love with him, that would put her at a distinct disadvantage.

She wouldn't let that happen.

"Mama. Mama," Kole called, holding his arms out to her. She had just taken a waffle out of the waffle iron, and she had the cup in her hand to pour more in.

"Hang on a second, bud. Mom is busy."

She smiled a little because Denver didn't exactly look comfortable with the children in his arms, but he did look good.

"Good morning, you two," she said over her shoulder to the kids he was holding as she poured the waffle batter in the pan. "There's a booster seat for Sky and a high chair for Kole." She nodded her head in the general direction of where they were.

Denver went easily, finding them and setting Sky down to grab her seat.

She didn't know what he did for living, but he didn't seem to flounder around which made her think that he was used to problem solving and figuring things out himself.

She probably ought to find out what he did, where he was going, and what kind of life they would have.

Was he quitting his job to farm? There was so much she didn't know.

They needed to have a long talk, but when?

Maybe after the kids went to bed tonight.

Her mind was brought back to the present when she heard what sounded like scratching in the mudroom.

That was weird. But she wasn't too concerned about it. She'd learned a long time ago, the night they'd moved in actually, that the house made all kinds of strange noises, and she'd gotten used to them.

Still, scratching was new.

"Jack, would you please shut the mudroom door?" she said as she pulled another waffle off the iron. "And, Ramona, can you grab the milk? Maggie, you can get the syrup."

Sky walked around, wanting to help, too.

"Maggie, can you please hand the butter to Sky, and, Sky, you can set it on the table."

She'd just poured batter on the iron when Jack said, "I think there's something out there." He opened the door.

After that, everything kind of happened in a blur.

Some kind of gray and black striped creature rushed in, hissing and knocking into things. It didn't seem to be able to see. Natalie didn't think of that until later. It was just the idea that there was something wild in her kitchen.

Maggie had been in the process of pulling the milk out.

Seeing the animal must have scared her, because she dropped it. The carton had been full, and falling from that height made it splatter all over the kitchen.

She must have bumped the ketchup while she was at it. Natalie always bought the big family-size ketchup, and it splattered and exploded on the floor with the milk as well.

That was the least of her worries, since there was an animal loose. The thought that it might have rabies sent chills down her spine.

There was a lot of yelling and noise and splattering going on, and even if the animal wasn't sick, it'd probably be crazy with fear.

Natalie was frozen for a second, then she started trying to figure out how she could save her children.

She had too many kids for her hands.

Sky was the closest to the animal. She was too young to understand the danger. She headed toward it, her hand out, not realizing what the hissing meant.

Natalie's heart galloped in her chest. A cold sweat broke out all over her body as her stomach lurched and bounced.

Jack and Maggie tried to run away. They fell in the milk on the floor. They ended up crawling, along with Ramona, under the table.

Natalie had taken two steps toward Sky when she felt pressure on her arm.

"Here." Denver shoved Kole at her and rushed forward, the booster seat in one hand. A step later, he grabbed Sky with the other. In one smooth motion, he twisted her around and set her on his back.

Automatically, she gripped his neck with her hands and squeezed tight.

Natalie held the warm body of her little boy close. How could Denver breathe with Sky squeezing so hard?

He kept one hand behind him, keeping Sky on his back, and with the other hand, he swung the booster seat at the animal in the kitchen.

Normally, Natalie might have said maybe they could shoo it out.

But in this instance, with it looking so sick and confused, wobbling into things, and even the fact that it was in their house in broad daylight, just seemed odd.

Beyond all of that, she was much more concerned about keeping her children safe than she was about saving the life of an animal.

The kitchen floor was slick with milk and ketchup, but Denver was in his stocking feet, and that seemed to be an asset.

At least, his stance was sure as he smacked the animal a second time, and it lay still.

Natalie, seeing that her other three children were safe underneath the kitchen table, had pressed herself back against the counter, in front of the waffle iron.

As she looked at the animal in a heap on the floor, and then stared at the man who had killed it with her baby on his back, and cuddled the one on her arms, she tried to get her legs to quit shaking.

What was burning?

"Mom?" Jack said.

"Not right now, Jack, please." She was breathless. She hadn't even done anything. What would they have done if Denver hadn't been there?

There was a huge mess to clean up, but she wasn't even worried about it right then. She would never have been able to kill that animal.

She shouldn't say never. As a mom, she'd done a lot of things she would have said she couldn't have done before she did them.

She just needed a minute to get her heartbeat under control.

"Mom?"

"Just give me a minute, please, Jack." She still sounded breathless, and Kole squirmed in her arms.

She held him too tight. She was just so thankful everyone was safe.

She hadn't been this scared while the animal was there, but now the fear caught up to her, and her body felt weak.

The burning smell was getting stronger. Is that how animals smelled when they died?

Denver moved the booster seat in his hand and looked it over like maybe he was looking for blood or something.

"Mom!" Jack's voice held real fear. She had really been putting him off.

Her eyes went to her son under the table, his sisters cowering behind him. He'd crawled out some, and his eyes were wide, his finger pointing.

Maggie had her hand over her mouth, and her eyes were wide too.

Natalie wasn't sure what it was, but she wouldn't have been the slightest bit surprised if Bigfoot had been standing behind her.

"What is it, honey?" She tried to sound calm and even maybe a bit serene; ideally, she would like to sound unaffected as well. The reality was it came out kind of shrew-like. To be honest.

Maybe it was her tone, maybe it was Jack's tone, or maybe the smell had finally gotten to him, but Denver looked up at the same time Jack said, "Mom, your hair is on fire."

DENVER HADN'T WANTED to kill the animal in front of the children, but he hadn't been able to figure out any other way of dealing with it. It wasn't cognizant enough to be chased or herded or guided anywhere. If it didn't have rabies, there was definitely something else wrong with it.

Thankfully, being that he'd been on a ship a good part of the last fifteen years, he didn't have too much trouble keeping his feet on the slick floor. Milk wasn't too much different than water.

The ketchup did add a different dimension to it, though. He'd never worked in ketchup before.

Jack called out that Natalie's hair was on fire almost the same instant he saw it himself. She'd been leaning back against the counter and it had apparently been touching the open waffle iron which had been hot enough to cause it to burst into flames.

He dropped the booster seat and rushed toward her, trying to yank his button-down out from under the child on his back and over his head as he went.

He thought Natalie was gonna drop the baby on the floor, and he understood. She didn't want him near the fire.

"Hold on. I've got this."

He eased the child from his back, setting her down. Thankfully, he hated feeling strangled, so he hadn't buttoned the top two buttons when he put his shirt on and it came over his head easily. The fire snuffed out almost as soon as he reached around her and put it on top of her hair.

He could feel her trembling, or maybe it was him.

His job was dangerous, sure. But usually he got to eat first.

This husband and father thing might be a little bit more difficult than he was first thinking.

Natalie tried to pull back, and he let his shirt fall, but he put his arm under Kole, either to take him or support him, whichever Natalie chose.

But the way she was shaking, he felt like she needed to go sit down.

Instead, her shoulders went up then down, and she leaned into him.

He slid his hand the rest of the way around her back, pulling her close. "So...is this a typical Sunday morning? Or did you guys think I might be bored if we just sat down at the table and ate breakfast?"

Her shoulders jiggled, like maybe she was laughing. He wasn't sure. "I guess, if you want to change your mind, there's still time. Although, this isn't exactly typical. Maybe the milk and ketchup on the floor is pretty normal."

He laughed. "So you don't usually kill your breakfast before you eat it in the morning?"

"No. No, that's new."

"Good to hear it. I'm kind of all about buying my meat at the store. I think marriages should be based on shared principles. Kinda glad we're in agreement on that one."

"Me too. Hopefully we're also in agreement that we're not actually going to eat that thing?"

"Yep. We are compatible."

Her head nodded. Then she leaned back and looked up. "Thank you. I keep thinking I don't know what we would have done if you hadn't been here, but I guess I don't need to wonder about that. Do I? God didn't give us a wild animal in our kitchen until he gave us you to handle it. I like how He works."

Her eyes were sparkling, and her smile big, even if it did tremble a little at the corners. He liked the show of humor and bravery. It was a good mixture, and he also liked that she was willing to lean on him some, too.

"You're welcome. It's not every day I get to turn a booster seat into a killing machine and go to war for my lady."

"Is that what happened?"

"Hey, it's my story, I'll tell it how I want to."

"Okay. I like your version."

The kids came slowly out from underneath the kitchen table, creeping around the edge of the kitchen, their eyes on the dead raccoon on the floor, like they were afraid it was going to come back to life again. When they got to Natalie and him, they wrapped their arms around their waists and pressed in tight.

He held them all for a little bit. Is this what it felt like to have a family? This weird, warm thing in his chest that made him feel strong and needed and loved and wanted.

He hadn't wanted the kids to see him kill the animal, but he didn't think they felt like they'd seen death. At least he didn't think they did. He got the impression that what they saw was him protecting them.

An odd way for family bonding to take place, but hey, he wasn't complaining. It all worked out well.

After a few minutes, he said, "If we don't get out and get moving, we're going to be late for church."

"You're right." Natalie backed off, then she gasped, and her hand went to her head. "How bad is it?" She'd forgotten about her hair.

He had to bite back a grin. Just feeling how good it felt to be almost like a family.

He flexed his jaw and scrunched his eyes up as he peered around.

"Maybe...maybe we should skip church today," he suggested slowly. "I think you'd look good in one of those short little," he put his finger up to his hair and kind of twirled it around, searching for the word to use, not that he could define girls' haircuts, "that short haircut that is kinda like a boy cut?" he ended as her mouth slowly opened, her jaw dropped, and her eyes widened, leaving her looking horrified. "You're not allowed to get more upset about your hair than you are about the kitchen with the dead animal in it. We have to remain compatible." He didn't say this in a commanding tone; it was more hopeful, with a little humor, hoping she would go with it.

He hadn't been around too many women, but he was pretty sure every single one he'd ever been around, including his sisters, was pretty attached to her hair. Emotionally, as well as literally. In fact, completely attached.

"I'm not sure I can joke about my hair right now," Natalie said. "I was supposed to be getting married this week sometime. I'm not sure if my husband-to-be will still want to marry me if I look like a boy."

"Well, you didn't ask for my opinion, but I can tell you with certainty your husband will still want to marry you, especially if you can laugh about it."

Yeah, she smiled. "I guess it's just hair. It'll grow back."

"It sure will. And eventually it will smell better too."

She wrinkled her nose, her cheeks pink. "It does kinda stink, doesn't it?"

"It does." As though to punctuate that, his stomach growled.

Natalie sighed, lines appearing between her brows. She bit her lip. "I'm not sure how to start with this mess," she said as she looked around. "It'd be nice if we can keep from tracking it through the house."

"How about I take the animal out, and I'll take my clothes off outside. There's a shower downstairs, and I'll get in it."

"That sounds good. If you tell me where your clothes are, I'll get you some to put on when you're done and set them outside the door," Natalie said, her tone sounding a little more in control. "Maggie, how about you, Ramona, and Sky take your things off and go upstairs and get in the tub." She turned and looked at Jack. "You wait until Mr. Denver is done, and then it will be your turn. Don't leave the kitchen, okay?"

Jack nodded, looking like he was back to his normal self as well. "Maybe I can go out with Mr. Denver and take care of the animal?"

"You sure can," Denver said before Natalie could turn him down. If he were going to be part of the family, he needed to get to know the kids. "I'll see if I can call the game commission; they might want to get it and test it."

Natalie looked a little surprised, but she didn't say anything.

"And in the meantime, Kole, who is the only one of us that doesn't have ketchup and milk all over him, can sit in his high chair."

"And I'll work on getting the mess cleaned up."

"Once I'm out of the shower, I'll take over and you can get the kids out and get yourself cleaned up."

She nodded. "And then I guess we give breakfast another shot. Since somebody is hungry." She looked at his stomach, which had growled again.

"Hey, I'm not used to all this excitement," he eyed the raccoon, "and danger."

"I'm glad we can give you your adrenaline rush for the day. Hopefully the rest of the day will be very calm. Maybe we'll put some Christmas music on, and hopefully we'll have a very boring afternoon."

Chapter Seventeen

Natalie stared at the blinking Christmas lights on the Christmas tree in her living room.

Well, it wasn't exactly her living room. Not yet. But she was supposed to get married this week sometime, although they hadn't set a date.

The second time they'd attempted breakfast, it had gone well. No wild animals, no liquids on the floor, and no fires. Any one of those would make for a good breakfast, but all three at once? She could hardly believe her luck.

No, her blessing. She could hardly believe her blessings.

What kind of man didn't get angry or at least upset or annoyed over everything that had happened this morning? She wasn't even going to start comparing Denver to her ex.

There really was no comparison, but he'd have been yelling at everybody. Not to mention, he probably would have expected *her* to kill the animal.

They'd gotten cleaned up, but they hadn't gone to church.

Instead, Denver had tried cutting her hair. Just getting the burned ends off.

He said he was pretty good at shaving guys' heads, but she declined to have a buzz cut. At least until she found out whether or not it was salvageable.

He said he'd marry her anyway, and she thanked him but still declined.

It had been fun.

Who'd have thought she could actually have fun?

They were going to get a tree, but they decided to work for a few hours.

She put the little ones to bed and shaped trees with the bush clippers he'd found. He'd cut trees down and shook them and wrapped them. She felt like they had a good jump on tomorrow, and they'd gotten more done today than they had Saturday morning when they'd still been figuring out what they needed to do. They were planning on getting up in the morning and working some more before customers came.

On the one hand, she thought they might be jinxing things if they got too much stuff ready; maybe no one would come. Still, it was nice to be prepared.

It'd been a nice day, and they'd gone together once the little children had gotten up to pick out a tree. Denver had shaken it, and they'd wrapped it too, which made it easier to get in and get set up.

Natalie didn't have any decorations, but there had been some in the attic of the old house, and they used those. They were kind of slapdashed together, but as she stood, the windows dark, the house silent, the lights on the tree just sparkling, and the ornaments reflecting that sparkle, she thought about the day, feeling warm and happy.

Hopeful. Excited about their future. For the first time in a really long time.

She couldn't really believe the way the Lord was working things out.

"It's not the most beautiful Christmas tree I've ever seen, but I'm a little bit proud of it. And kind of protective." Denver padded in on stocking feet and stopped beside her. Plenty of distance between them.

She glanced over. "Me too."

"More of this compatibility stuff that's supposed to be good for marriages. I like it."

She grinned. He seemed to be able to do that to her pretty easily. She nodded. "We're practically twins."

"That's what I was thinking. Pretty soon we'll be finishing—"

"—each other's sentences," she said, and they laughed together.

"I just came back down because I want to tell you I had a good time today."

"I did too. Thank you. I was just marveling at how God works things out sometimes." She thought about Welder Man.

Maybe talking to him had prepared her for Denver, since Denver just seemed so familiar. Like a man cut from the same cloth.

He hadn't emailed her at all, and after that first time, she had never emailed him first.

It was probably better that way. Although a little piece of her wondered where he was and what he was doing and if he were okay.

"I could marvel at the same thing." He too seemed lost in thought. She figured she might as well ask the question that had kind of been in the back of her mind.

Staring at the lights, like it didn't matter to her one way or the other, she said, "Are you sure that you're not going to find a woman that you could fall in love with someday and regret this?" Her voice was soft and gentle. She wasn't sure she wanted to know the answer, but she didn't want to accuse him of anything either.

"I'm sure. I think a lot of life is denying your feelings and doing what's right."

That wasn't really what she wanted to hear.

She watched the lights, enjoying the sparkle.

"I also think love is more of an action. I don't know if there are any tingly feelings that last. I know I had two examples of great marriages, and I really want to have one like them."

"Two?"

"Race and Penny adopted my siblings and me after our birth parents were killed in a car accident. My parents had a great marriage, and so do Race and Penny. I don't think it's based on tingly feelings but more of an attitude and a determination to stay together and to make your lives together fun and happy." He slanted a look at her as though to judge her reaction to his words. They weren't typical.

She kind of wanted the tingly feelings, to be honest. She bit her lip and looked down. Could she tell him that?

"You disagree?" he asked softly.

She nodded a little. And then turned to face him. "I guess I don't disagree as much as I would rather have both."

He turned to face her and took a step toward her. "Both? You want everything?"

"You don't always get what you want. But yeah, if I could choose, I'd have both."

She swallowed, not feeling nearly as confident as her words sounded. He didn't intimidate her exactly, though he was bigger than she was, but it was more that he had such an advantage over her. The house was his, the farm was his, it was in his power to throw her out or to say no, and she would have no place to go for herself and her kids. She didn't want to make him angry.

But she didn't want to agree to something that she didn't agree with.

"And how does that look to you?" His voice had lowered, and there was almost a caress in it.

It drew her. She took a step closer. "I guess that looks a little bit like it did today. Where we have fun together. But maybe...maybe affection? Maybe it's not a 'can't keep my hands off you,' necessarily, but admiration? Maybe appreciation?"

He took the last step and lifted his hand, running it along the hair above her ear, pushing it back. "I can't disagree with any of that. I do think, though, with the right actions, the right feelings follow."

She nodded, because her mouth had gone dry. His thumb traced the outside edge of her ear.

"Is this affection?" he asked.

"For me." She nodded. Swallowing, she asked, "What about you?"

"No. I don't think so."

Her face scrunched. "No?"

He shook his head. "I don't think we're nearly close enough for me to term this affection."

She smiled a little. "Well, we haven't known each other very long, but we're very compatible. I suppose, being that it's Christmas and all, we could get closer."

"Blame it on Christmas?" There was definitely humor in his voice.

She nodded. And inched forward, just a little more.

His fingers buried in her hair, and she grimaced because of the shortness and the ugliness.

"What? Am I hurting you?" His hand came out and wrapped around her neck.

"No. It's just...I feel ugly." Especially compared to him. No one wanted to stand beside perfection and be found wanting.

"You're not," he said, soft and fierce.

She wasn't going to argue. He'd said they were close enough, so she reached out and slid both hands around his waist. "Affection?"

"Maybe we found something we're not compatible with," he said, the humor in his tone still there but more subdued,

"Oh?"

"I think this is affection." He leaned down and brushed his lips along her forehead. A soft touch that made all the tingly feelings fall around her like glitter.

"And this." He kissed the edge of her jaw.

More glitter.

"And this is affection too." His lips touched the edge of her mouth. A sweet touch, and soft, and her whole body felt warm all around. She closed her eyes.

"What are you thinking?" he asked.

"I have the tingly feelings." She smiled without opening her eyes.

"You're saying you have it all?"

She nodded. Opening her eyes, she moved her head and touched her lips to the edge of his chin. "Affection?"

He nodded. A little smile as well, although his eyes were hooded.

She reached out, standing on her tiptoes, and touched her lips to the corner of his mouth. "Affection?"

He nodded again. "I don't think it's very manly to admit to tingly feelings. But if you promise not to tell anyone, I have it all too."

She smiled. "Compatibility."

"Practically twins."

"You know, it's weird, but I feel so comfortable with you. Like we've known each other a lot longer."

"Same." His thumb brushed over her cheek. "Although there's a certain tension in my stomach when I'm this close to you. It doesn't exactly feel comfortable."

She almost giggled. "I make you nervous?"

"Maybe. Maybe I'm worried you'll come to your senses and realize you're too good for me and walk away."

She laughed outright at that. "That's funny. I'm the one with five children. And burnt hair. And the one who's been handed all of her dreams on the silver platter when you walked in and asked me to marry you."

"Really? All your dreams?"

"Every single one."

"I'm not sure I can do adoration here in the living room in front of God and everybody. But I can definitely do more affection." He pulled her hand up and kissed her palm. And then cupped it around his cheek.

"I'm good with more affection. But...everybody?"

He grinned. "I don't know much about kids, but I think they usually come in at the most inopportune times."

"That's all you need to know about kids. And it's the truth."

"I didn't do a very good job of asking you to marry me the first time. Can I have a do-over?"

"A do-over?" Her heart started pounding slow and hard in her chest. What was he talking about?

He took the hand that he'd been holding to his cheek and gripped it in his fingers, slowly lowering to one knee. He reached in his pocket and pulled out a ring.

"I... I'll try to show you that I love you. An act of love. I know I won't have a problem with affection." One side of his lip tilted up. "I know I have the tingles down too. I know we talked about a marriage of convenience. Marriage is still marriage to me. That means I'll spend my life devoted to you. Would you marry me?"

Natalie blinked back tears. She hadn't expected a marriage proposal at all and certainly not one that romantic.

Unsuccessful at holding back her tears, she tried to brush them aside.

"Same?" she said, meaning to say it with purpose and surety, but it came out on a wobble. It wasn't a question that she was asking him if she felt the same; she was asking him if it was okay if she just said "same" rather than any other words that she couldn't form.

He grinned. "It's a good thing I don't need all those pretty words."

She willed her throat to unclench, tried to force the words out. "I'm sorry. You gave me such a beautiful speech, and I gave you nothing. It's kind of the way I feel our whole relationship is. You've given me everything, and I don't understand what you're getting out of it."

He ran his hand over her fingers, looking at them. "I'm getting someone who gives me tingles."

She laughed.

"Someone to lie beside me at night and wake up beside me in the morning. I'm getting someone who laughs at rabid raccoons in their kitchen and doesn't cry when their hair catches on fire. Someone who loves her children and protects them first. Who will warm food up for me at eleven o'clock at night and put it on the table and keep me company while I eat it. Who works alongside me and makes me laugh. Who will grow old with me, and we'll have fun together while we do it."

He brought her fingers up and touched his lips to the end of one. Then he looked up at her. "None of those are things that money can buy. None of those are things that are easy to come by. I think I'm the one who's blessed."

He kissed another finger and nipped it with his teeth, and glitter exploded again.

"You never gave me an answer."

"I'd be a fool to say anything but yes."

He started to slide the ring on her finger.

"Where'd you get that?"

"My brother West was here yesterday. He was there on Thanksgiving. He'd heard what Dad was saying to me, and I guess, when my parents died, I never noticed, but West took the engagement ring off my mother's finger. It had been her grandmother's. She'd always said she wanted us kids to have it. One of us. She never said which one.

"I was out talking with Dad on the porch, and West asked the rest of the kids if it was okay if he gave it to me. Do you mind wearing my great-grandmother's ring?"

"I'm honored."

"I think it almost fits."

"I think so too."

"Thinking some affection might be in order."

"Denver?"

"Hmm?"

"If you want to kiss me, go ahead."

"How did you know?"

"Maybe that's because that's what I want too?"

"You're beautiful when you smile."

"You're handsome all the time. And your hair is not burned. So there's that."

"I don't care about your hair. I told you we could shave it off."

"I care about yours." She smirked at him.

"Man, if I'd known how shallow she was, maybe I'd have picked a different girl."

"You didn't pick me, I got forced on you, remember?"

They grinned at each other. Maybe they weren't exactly romantic words, but it felt like a personal joke.

"Best thing that ever happened to me. Think I just told you that."

"And I don't care about your hair. You know what, we could just end this controversy, and we can go bald together. We'll be the bald Christmas tree sellers."

"I'm fine with that. I'm losing it anyway. Maybe that's why I'm marrying you, because I figured I'd better get married before I go fully bald."

"I don't care how bald you are. Or honestly what you look like. As long as you can kill every rabid raccoon that ever walks in my kitchen, I'll take you."

He laughed. "No pressure. I might not have a booster seat in my hand the next time."

"At least our kids will have good stories to tell anyway." They smiled at each other.

"That they will." He squeezed her hand. "I was kinda thinking, maybe there will be a rainy day this week, so we don't lose any day selling trees, and we can go to the courthouse and get a license. There's no waiting period, so as soon as we have it, we can get married. Dad'll do it anytime, I'm sure. Does that sound good to you? Do you have a preference for your day?"

She shook her head. "However it works out is how it works out. I've been trying to live that way. Just trust in the Lord to work things out." She looked him up and down and grinned. "He's done pretty good by me so far."

"Woman, you need higher standards." He took her hand. "Come on. We've got a lot of work to do tomorrow. Let's go to bed."

Chapter Eighteen

onday turned out to be another exceptionally busy day.

Customers didn't start arriving until after lunch, but they'd spent the morning getting trees ready, shaping them, cutting them, and wrapping them, so they were a little more prepared when people showed up.

They were so busy there were a couple of hours in the evening when Denver could barely stop to breathe.

He kept a better eye on Natalie, though.

It wasn't hard, because she was on his mind constantly.

He wanted to find out what she'd been doing all summer. As they were waiting for their tree, several people had made comments about the fruit stand and asked him about fruit for next year.

He hadn't known, and didn't know, and couldn't answer.

By the time Natalie came over and held her hands out for Kole, he could admit he was getting tired. Kole had seemed pretty happy spending most of the evening riding around on his shoulders. Denver hadn't missed Natalie's concerned glances across the space that separated them throughout the evening either.

He wasn't sure whether that was concern for Kole or him.

Maybe both.

Jack had been his shadow, and the kid was a good help. Respectful as well. Denver enjoyed having him around.

Natalie had been in the house for two hours as Denver finished up with the stragglers and took some inventory for the next morning.

He was just about ready to shut the pole lights off and go to the house when Natalie, wearing a long flowing skirt and a coat zipped up to her chin, a beanie hat on her head, and her curly hair flowing out from underneath it, stepped out of the house and started walking down.

There was no spring in her step, but she walked with confidence, although as she got closer, he could see the lines of exhaustion around her face.

Not for the first time, he wondered why she was doing this.

No one was making her. And yeah, they were going to get married now, but back before they'd decided that, she had worked just as hard. Why?

She carried a thermos, too. He flipped the pole lights off and started walking toward her.

"Thank you," he said as she held the thermos out.

"It's hot chocolate. I wasn't sure whether you would drink coffee this late."

"I'll drink coffee anytime. But hot chocolate is warm and wet, and I'm grateful. Thank you."

She smiled a little. "I'll keep that in mind. Coffee tomorrow night."

"We could bring a coffee maker down."

Her brows lifted, and she got a pensive look on her face, like she'd never thought of that before. "That's a great idea."

"You know, we'll have all winter to talk about it, but I can see this becoming something a lot bigger than just selling trees."

She nodded. "I've had so many ideas too. I just don't have

enough time to do everything. I'm just trying to keep my head above water selling what we have and watching the kids."

"Next year, they'll be a year older. Jack's a great help. Thanks for letting him stay with me tonight."

She laughed a little. "Thanks for keeping him. I tried to make sure that he wasn't in your way. You know you can always send him back to me if he is."

"I didn't mind. He was a good help. And I'm not expecting him to be perfect. I can put up with a few mistakes from Jack as long as you all can put up with a few mistakes out of me. Maybe more than a few."

"We'll put up with anything. Well..." Her face clouded. "Almost anything."

She looked away, like she didn't want to go there, and he thought about Mom of Five and her story with her abusive husband.

He should probe further into Natalie's past. But it was so late, and they were both exhausted. She probably didn't want to dredge up bad memories before she went to bed anyway.

"It's supposed to be nice tomorrow too. First rain is forecast for Thursday."

"I saw that. Only my phone said Friday."

"We could plan on Friday afternoon? I set it up with Jonathan that he's gonna be stopping in and picking me up. Probably around three o'clock Friday."

She nodded. "Thanks for letting me know."

"If there's no rain before that, we'll get married Friday at lunchtime, and maybe we'll grab a bite to eat." He wasn't sure how she'd feel if he said they'd have a last meal out together before he left. Like it was a goodbye party.

Was she fond enough of him to miss him when he left? Or would it be a relief?

He suspected, by the time he was done working with Natalie all week, he wouldn't want to be leaving.

"How long did you say you're going to be gone?" she asked, her voice sounding kind of soft and a little insecure. Maybe she was going to miss him.

"A week. That should put me back a week before Christmas."

"Okay." She took a deep breath but didn't look at him, almost like she was trying to hide the fact that she was fortifying herself.

"Why don't you see if you can find someone to come out and handle this with you? I mean, neither one of us knows whether it's going to get more or less busy."

"Journee might help me. She did come out some this summer. We work well together."

"Okay." He debated for a second. "I can say something to Dad, too. Oftentimes, there's someone in the church who needs a job. He wouldn't send anyone out here he wasn't sure was trustworthy, or he might come out with them himself." He put a hand on her arm. "I don't want you to be out here with someone you're not comfortable with, and if you're not comfortable with that idea, it's totally up to you."

She didn't look excited about it. Her lip was pulled in, and he thought she might be chewing on her cheeks as well.

"Can I think about it?" she finally asked.

"Of course. I won't say anything more. If you decide you want me to say something, you come to me. That way you don't feel pressured."

Her eyes held relief when she looked at him. "Thank you."

He had kissed her last night, not properly, but he'd wanted to.

He wanted to again tonight. But she looked tired. And he was leaving.

"What do you say we go to the house, and I'll get myself something to eat?"

"I already have your shepherd's pie warming up in the oven. That's part of the reason I came down, I wanted to know how long it was going to be, because I didn't want to burn it. It's probably done now."

A feeling that he couldn't explain expanded in his chest. He wasn't used to anyone taking care of him. The few women that he'd worked with really had to be tough in order to work in the kinds of jobs he did. They were just as likely to tell him to shove it where the sun didn't shine if he'd asked them to make him something to eat. Which he never had. He only had to see them say that to someone else once. He'd never made that mistake.

He supposed women like that were great on the job, but as he turned and walked toward the house, he put his arm around Natalie's shoulders. They might be nice to work with, but they weren't who he wanted to be walking into his house with at the end of the day. He wanted someone exactly like Natalie.

He just hoped he could be to her what she was becoming for him.

TUESDAY WAS BUSY, if uneventful. Natalie didn't mind uneventful.

Not when eventful meant toilets that didn't work, rabid raccoons in the kitchen, and messes that took her hours to clean up.

After he replaced the toilet Monday morning, they fell into a routine, working on the trees in the morning, struggling to get enough ready to go so that they wouldn't run out in the evening, and then selling into the night, with her taking the children around eight, giving them baths, and putting them to bed.

Wednesday, though, something happened that she thought might be an answer to a prayer.

Denver had mentioned having someone from the church come out and help her. She was okay with that, except she preferred it to be someone she was comfortable being around the children.

She and Journee worked really well together, and Journee was patient with her children. If it were just her, she might not be so picky.

But she couldn't keep an eye on the kids every single second, and she didn't want to worry about them being around anyone she didn't trust.

She'd been working for hours, chatting with customers, when she gradually became aware that there was a curvy woman with dark brown hair standing off the side, as though she were waiting on something.

Natalie was in the middle of checking out a customer who was getting not one but five Christmas trees and seemed to have brought the entire family with her and most of her neighbors, too.

It was another ten minutes before Natalie could look over again. When she did, the woman was now sitting on the floor, with Sky on one knee and Ramona on the other and grimy little-girl fingerprints on her cheeks.

The fingerprints surprised Natalie because when she had thought the word curvy, she hadn't meant heavyset. She'd meant lots of curves on the top, with lots of curves on the bottom, and a tightly nipped waist in between.

Kind of like a Barbie doll.

Natalie didn't know anything about plastic surgery, but the figure didn't look quite realistic to her.

The lashes also looked thick and dark, even in the dim light.

The woman was conservatively dressed with a loose shirt under a fur-lined vest and loose, boot-cut jeans.

Still, there was just something about her that didn't say "local."

Natalie wondered if she had the same vibe about her. Although she'd grown up in a small town just like this.

This woman didn't say "small town," either.

The lady and her entourage with five Christmas trees were finally checked out, and she took a minute to take a few steps over and then bend down on her knees in front of the woman.

She held her hand out. "I'm Natalie. Can I help you?"

The woman's smile revealed a mouthful of the whitest teeth Natalie had ever seen. Normally, thoughts like that didn't run through her head, but the first thing she thought was: *Are they real?*

Nothing about the woman looked real.

It wasn't a judgment, necessarily; it was just Natalie had really never seen anyone like her.

The woman reached from behind Sky's back and held out her hand. "I'm Bun... Burgundy. It's a pleasure to meet you."

Her voice sounded just a tad rough but cultured. It held a note of insecurity, at odds with everything, like she wasn't sure whether Natalie was going to accept her hand and allow her to continue to hold her children.

Odd.

Still, she didn't have a bad feeling about the woman. On the contrary. Any woman who would sit on the ground and allow two dirty little kids to climb all over her was someone who made Natalie comfortable.

"Excuse me? Can you wait on me tonight?" A woman's impatient voice cut through Natalie's thoughts.

"Did you need me?" Natalie asked Burgundy without looking at the lady who'd just hollered at her.

The woman's mouth turned up in a lopsided, almost self-effacing grin. "Looks like you're needed elsewhere. I can wait."

Natalie's brows drew down a little, wondering what the woman wanted, but she nodded. "Thanks."

The line of customers was at least ten people long when Natalie turned back around.

"I'm sorry. Can I help you?" she said to the lady at the counter.

"I want to return this tree. It doesn't look at my house the way it did in the field."

The words from the woman were kinda snippy, and Natalie was slightly taken aback. Like the woman was personally insulted that her Christmas tree didn't look the way she thought it should.

"I'm sorry." What should she do? She hadn't had this problem. Instinct took over. "Of course. We'll refund your money in full. Did you pay by cash or check?"

"I don't know. My husband got it."

"Oh?" How did the woman know that it didn't look like it did in the field then?

Still, she wasn't going to question the woman. But she wasn't going to refund her cash if she paid with a check.

"Can you get a hold of him and ask?" Natalie said politely.

"I can, but I'm not waiting. I want this taken care of immediately. I had to wait behind those people with the five Christmas trees, and I don't want you to put me off. I have things to do."

There was a line behind the woman, and Natalie was opening her mouth to say that she had other people to take care of, that the woman could wait or come back when they weren't so busy, but she felt a presence at her elbow.

Burgundy spoke from beside her. "If you don't mind, I'll take care of the people who are purchasing trees."

The woman could be a thief. She could end up stealing everything they made tonight.

Even as she thought that, Natalie dismissed the thought. Maybe she was a thief. Maybe she would steal. But they needed help, and she was going to take this chance.

She kind of thought that Denver would be okay with it. Although, the idea of Denver being around this woman made her slightly uneasy. She couldn't quite put her finger on why, and she hated that it felt like judgment on her part.

She shoved the feeling aside. The woman had been nothing but nice, and she still had dirt on her face.

"You have handprints on your face," Natalie said, putting a hand up to her own cheek to indicate where the dirt prints were on Burgundy's.

Burgundy laughed. "Thanks." She pulled her hand up and wiped at the porcelain white skin on her cheek.

"That's pretty good," Natalie said softly. "I appreciate your help."

Maggie was on the far end of the counter in front of a sign that said "Rent Your Saws HERE."

When she'd suggested that Jack and Maggie do that together,

Maggie had insisted she could do it herself, and Jack had said he wanted to be with Denver.

It worked out. Maggie was a natural, looking very prim and proper on her high stool behind the counter. She hadn't gotten bored and left, either.

Burgundy and Natalie worked side by side for two more hours before it was thirty minutes past time for her to take the kids up to the house.

That little nagging feeling in the back of her head about leaving Denver alone with Burgundy was the reason she was thirty minutes late.

Finally, she decided that she might as well find out now what was going to go on. She wasn't married yet.

Maybe it was the wedding fiasco that Denver's sister had had earlier in the summer, or maybe it was just her general distrust of men because of her husband.

Or maybe it was something about the woman that just felt off.

Whatever it was, the bigger feeling in her gut told her that she could trust Burgundy, and she absolutely, with a steadfast assurance, knew she could trust Denver.

It was just her past rising up.

She thought.

"Are you okay here? I really appreciate your help, but it's time for my children to go to bed. Things have been slowing down, and I think you'll be okay here alone, although it'll be a little bit busy for another half an hour or so."

"I'll be fine. Are you sure?" It was like Burgundy herself wasn't sure whether Natalie was actually going to trust her or not.

It took Natalie a couple of moments of looking at Burgundy's eyes, dark with the long lashes and kind of sultry. But there was something about her, something that said that her appearance wasn't what it seemed.

"Yes. I'm sure."

As she had done the past few nights they'd worked together,

Natalie fed the children, gave the kids baths, got them ready for bed, and read them a story, doing their normal nighttime routine, before she went downstairs and put some food back for Denver.

She put coffee in a thermos and started out of the house.

Her foot hadn't even touched the steps of the porch when she saw that all the cars were gone, and Denver was doing inventory and cleaning things up, alone.

Somehow, he always seemed to know when she was approaching, because she hadn't been on the driveway more than ten yards when he looked up.

It always made him smile to see her. Which made her heart sing.

He wrote a note on the notepad, shoved it under the counter, shut the lights off, and started walking toward her.

Maybe it was her imagination, but he seemed to be walking eagerly, like he couldn't wait to get to her.

She had to admit her own steps picked up, and some of her tiredness eased. There was just something about having a man look at her like that.

No. Not a man, Denver. Having Denver look at her like that. With a smile, and an eagerness to see her, and his desire to be with her.

It made her feel special in a way she never had before. Made her feel like she didn't have five kids. Made her feel she hadn't totally screwed her life up. Made her feel...loved.

Even though he'd never said the word.

"Something warm and wet, and carried by someone sweet and thoughtful, thank you," he said when they met and she held out the thermos.

His words made her smile. How could she not?

"You're welcome."

He unscrewed the lid and took a drink.

"Who was the woman that was with you today?" he asked.

"Her name is Burgundy. I don't know anything more about her. She was a great help, though, and I appreciated it."

Denver nodded. "She left before I could say anything to her. I just looked around, when the last car pulled out, and she was gone."

Natalie nodded. The woman didn't seem to be after Denver. Just something about her look said that she might have been.

"I think things were busier tonight than they've been all week," Natalie said as they started walking slowly up to the house together.

Denver took her hand. He'd done it the previous evening too, and she liked it.

It was still new enough that their eyes met when he took it, and they smiled at each other. Soft smiles, communicating without words.

"I think you might be right."

If he was thinking what she was—that they only had one more day together—he didn't say. She tried not to let that thought ruin their evening as he ate and they talked and then went to bed in their separate rooms.

Thursday afternoon, Burgundy appeared again.

This time, she didn't sit on the floor with the kids, although when Sky came over to her leg and patted it, Burgundy bent and picked her up.

There was some kind of sadness and longing in her eyes that hurt Natalie's heart and also made her curious about her past.

But Burgundy was great with customers, and people seemed to love her, especially Sky and Ramona.

When Natalie was ready to take the children, she tried to talk to Burgundy, just a little more. "Do you live in Mistletoe?"

"Just about a mile or so outside of it."

Natalie nodded, trying to figure out what else she could ask that wouldn't be too nosy.

Burgundy patted her hair, like it was habit more than she was concerned how it looked. "Pastor Race told me there might be a job out here..." Her full lips pursed. "Is there?"

The pause before she asked the question seemed almost like she was gathering up her nerve. Like she was afraid of the rejection.

"There sure is. Denver," she nodded her head over toward where Denver was shaking the trees and wrapping them, "is leaving for a week, and I could really use the help."

"You can count on me."

It seemed almost too good to be true. But Natalie wasn't going to look a gift horse in the mouth. "If it's raining tomorrow, we're going to stay closed. We'll be closed anyway until at least four o'clock."

Denver had said his buddy was coming at three.

"Thank you." Burgundy's body seemed to relax.

"I'll have some paperwork that you'll need to fill out, but I don't have it with me today. We'll do it tomorrow. Or Saturday, if it's raining."

"Thank you. I'll do my best to do a good job."

"You're doing a great job so far. I appreciate it."

Chapter Nineteen

Was rain a bad omen for a wedding?

Denver held the hand of his new wife and considered the question. Sky was in his other arm, and Natalie held Kole. They'd been holding them through the ceremony too. It was thankfully short.

His dad looked happy, his mom a little worried as he slipped the thick gold band on Natalie's finger.

He'd gotten one for himself, too, and he wore it now.

They walked out of his parents' home and jogged quickly down the sidewalk through what felt like a monsoon.

He wanted to open the door for his new wife; it seemed like the least he could do. But they were trying to get the kids in as quickly as they could, without getting them wet, so he went to his side while she went to hers.

Natalie deserved a little more romance than that in her life. He wanted to give it to her.

Not that he was a great romantic. Because he really wasn't. But it just seemed to him she could use it.

He could be wrong, but he thought maybe she hadn't been cherished very much in her life.

He wanted to do that for his wife. Cherish her.

He just needed to figure out how.

The other kids got buckled, and they ended up plopping down in the front seats next to each other at the same time, slamming the doors against the rain. They looked across the console. Natalie had a little grin on her face, which eased his heart a little. This wasn't exactly the wedding of her dreams.

"I'd like to take you out for a steak dinner. That okay?"

Her smile had frozen on her face, and her eyes had blinked three or four times when he'd said "steak dinner."

The way she looked at him... Something triggered in his mind. Some memory.

His mouth hung open a little, and maybe he was staring at her too intently, because she shook her head a little and looked away.

"Yes," she said, staring at her hands in her lap. Her shoulders heaved up, and then she looked over at him. "Yes. That would be so nice."

He nodded, still feeling just a little odd. Like there was something he should know but didn't.

"Have you ever been to a steak house?" He wasn't sure where that question came from, other than he couldn't really figure out what else would cause her reaction. He still couldn't figure out what caused his.

She shook her head. Her shoulder came up. "Moms of young children don't go out too much, I'm afraid."

"Do you want to?" he asked, his voice kind of soft. He wasn't sure what it was about him that had shifted over the past week. Maybe it was because of her making sure he had hot coffee, making sure he had a hot meal after he came in at night. She'd done his laundry and cooked breakfast. She hadn't even asked. Little things that she did, just to make him more comfortable, and it had made him want to do the same for her.

"If you don't mind that the kids are tired and cranky?" Her eyes seemed to be a little worried, like he might actually care.

"They're kids. Hopefully they think this is a good day too. As I do." He looked over at her, and his words made her smile.

They ate at the steak house, and she was right. The kids were cranky. Not misbehaving, but just fussy.

He made a note, for when he got back, that they would go for a real date. His mom would watch the kids. She'd probably think it was a good thing, too.

He hadn't grown up with her, but she'd always been saying how important it was for men to take care of their women.

Old-fashioned, maybe. But it was definitely in his DNA to protect and provide. He didn't understand why it was so important to fight that.

Thankfully, he didn't think Natalie was the kind of woman that he'd have to fight it with. She seemed to like it when he tried to take care of her. In return, she was nurturing, and somehow the way she treated him made him feel like he could do anything.

He liked it.

It was five til three when they walked out of the steak house. He'd told his buddy where they were, and he'd packed his stuff. Natalie was going to drive home. Alone.

He didn't like it. Vowed it wouldn't happen again. Hated that they'd just gotten married and he wasn't even going home with her. Whether it was a marriage of convenience or not.

They stood just inside the doors, watching the rain come down in sheets. It was going to be another mad dash through the parking lot and no lingering goodbye.

Kole fussed in his arms, grabbing at his hair and pulling. Thankfully, his hair was short, and Kole couldn't get a hold.

"Thanks for eating with me. I'm sorry I have to leave." It was stupid to wait until Friday to get married. Now he had to leave her with five kids to take care of on her own. Five cranky kids. Sky pulled on her arm on one side, and Ramona leaned against her front while Maggie and Jack argued about something behind them.

"That's life. I'm glad you have a job."

Her words struck him. She wasn't complaining, she wasn't whining, and she wasn't hanging onto him.

She wasn't begging him to stay. She just accepted it and looked at the positive. He didn't care if they were still standing in the restaurant, if the kids around them were fussing, and if Jonathan was outside waiting on him.

He stepped closer and put his hand on her cheek. "I don't deserve you."

She put her hand up over his, and something flashed across her eyes, something that made him realize that maybe she really didn't want him to go. That maybe everything she was doing was a brave front.

He appreciated it all the more.

"I'm not anything special."

The kids bounced around them, and a couple squeezed by, murmuring, "Excuse me." Denver didn't pay any attention to them.

He stepped closer to Natalie. "Sorry. I have to disagree. I can't explain how you make me feel."

She shook her head, still denying it. "I'm just a mom of five."

"And I'm just a welder..."

Their eyes met. Hers widening as dawning realization crept over her face.

His heart stopped. His fingers on her face curled. His eyes searched hers.

"Mom of Five?" He could barely get the words out.

"Welder Man?"

It was her. It was Natalie. Natalie was Mom of Five. He couldn't believe it. Couldn't believe he'd been so stupidly blind. Of course. All the pieces fit.

She hadn't sent Welder Man an email since he'd come.

He hadn't sent Mom of Five an email either.

They both were smiling.

"That's why you seem so familiar. That's why I kept feeling like I knew you." The steak house entryway was hardly the place, not for this conversation, but he couldn't stop it. "All the pieces fit. Can't believe I didn't see it."

"Me either. I can't believe it. I...I guess I feel so comfortable with you. And that's why."

A car horn blasted, and he jerked up. Jonathan sat outside, the rain pouring down, gesturing in the pickup.

His heart dipped and fell.

"That's my ride. I have to go. We're already gonna be late. Especially in this rain. But I'll help you get the kids in the car." It was the least he could do. He wanted to do more. Wanted to touch her and hold her and thank God for the blessing of getting everything he wanted and more.

"You don't have to." She reached out to take Kole from him.

"No. It's pouring. I'm not gonna let you go by yourself." He sighed. "You have no idea how much I don't want to leave." He shook his head and shoved the door open, holding it for everyone.

They ran to the car, which wasn't very far away. He waved at Jonathan as he ran by, and Jonathan motored after them, stopping behind her SUV.

He got Kole buckled, then ran around the car to Natalie where she was just finishing buckling Sky.

"I hate leaving. I hate it. I'm sorry," he said, loud enough to be heard over the pouring rain.

"We'll be fine. I'll email you." She smiled. A true, brilliant smile. And he wondered if she'd had the fight with herself that he had. She'd won it. She hadn't sent any emails.

He'd won it too.

She put both hands on his cheeks, the rain pouring down her face as she looked up at him. "Please. Please, be careful."

He'd told her about the sharks and the lines and the dangers... about Crew. Now she'd just worry.

"I'm always careful. I'm more worried about you."

"Don't be. You know I'll be fine."

"It's my job to take care of you. I can't do that when I leave."

"I don't want you to go. But I understand why you have to."

They stared at each other for a few moments, oblivious to the rain and the fact that they were both soaking wet. Finally, Jonathan tapped on the truck horn.

"I think he's in a hurry," Natalie said.

"I think he can wait. I'm going to kiss my wife goodbye."

Natalie's eyes brightened, glinting at him through the pouring rain.

He lowered his head. He didn't kiss her forehead, or jaw, or the side of her lips.

His mouth landed on hers, and her hands went around his shoulders and neck, urging him closer.

He pulled her tighter, lifting her up and pressing her against the side of her car, kissing her the way he'd wanted to for a long time.

Excitement at knowing who she was, happiness at having everything he'd wanted, wonder at the way the Lord had worked things out, frustration that he hadn't seen it before, and sweet passion that exploded between them...all clouded his brain, making him not care about the public parking lot they were in, and the rain coming down, and his friend waiting for him.

All he cared about was kissing his wife and hoping she was enjoying it just as much as he was.

He heard the car horn again and realized it was the third time Jonathan had laid on it, this time without letting up.

"I'm gonna have to put his dead body in the back of the pickup," he whispered as he lifted his lips from hers.

"It was the best kiss I've ever had, too," she whispered, with a little tease in her voice.

He laughed. "It might have been the best kiss I ever had. But I wasn't done. Wasn't nearly done."

He lowered his head again. Just before his lips touched Natalie's, Jonathan laid on the horn again.

"Is this embarrassing you?" he asked, vowing to himself that if she said yes, he'd stop.

"Just kiss me," she whispered.

Chapter Twenty

Dear Mom of Five,

I know I've only been gone for five minutes, but I had to write. I can't believe I'm married to you and didn't even know it.

I can't believe that God has given me such an amazing woman – a whole family.

I'm excited about our life together in a way I've never been about my job or work. I wish I didn't have to go. I can't wait to get back.

Write me. Please.

B mine,

Welder Man

PS Wow. That kiss. It took my heart.

Dear Welder Man,

I feel the exact same way! I never imagined things would turn out like this. Not in a million years. Who would have thought one wrong letter in an email would set me on a course like this?

By the way – I never sent another email. Obviously, God directed the first, then he convicted me about sending any more.

Please, please, please be so very careful. I want to hold on to you and protect you, but I know I have to leave that in God's hands.

It's hard.

See me with you,

Mom of Five

PS I promise, your heart is safe in my chest. Beating strong. Maybe that's why I spend my nights dreaming about your kiss?

Dear Mom of Five,

Thanks so much for having the kids write to me! What a surprise. Their letters were funny. I hope they enjoyed my replies.

I have to say, I liked their mother's letter better.

This crazy job won't ever end. It's going to be very close to Christmas until I get home, now.

A couple of things weren't put together right and something else broke. We've also had some bad weather – which is why the season for underwater welding is usually over by now. Just, this job needs done.

Don't worry. I've never had six reasons to be extremely safe waiting for me at home like I do now. You're in my head constantly.

Don't think for one second that I'm not going to be rushing home just as fast as I can once it's over. I miss you, lady, more than you can possibly know.

B with you soon,

Welder Man

PS Ah, it makes sense now. That's your heart in my chest and that explains why I can't stop thinking about you, can't stop thanking God for you, can't stop wanting to be with you and I really can't stop thinking about that kiss that I wasn't nearly finished with.

Dearest Welder Man,

Don't think about rushing home. Please focus on being safe. That's all I care about. I would much rather wait and have you unhurt, than rush and have something happen. Please?

You wouldn't believe the Christmas trees we're selling. I had no idea they would be so popular. And, apparently, the previous owner sold truckloads of trees to stores in the area. They also shipped some out. I donated a truckload to the Mistletoe Volunteer Fire Company for them to sell as a fundraiser. I hope that was okay?

See you safe.

Mom of Five

PS The beginning of that kiss was spectacular. I can't imagine what the end could be like. I'm dreaming of it.

Dearest Natalie,

I'm sorry I'm going to miss Christmas. This is my last job. Ever. Man, if I thought there was any chance of me making it to shore, I'd be jumping off and swimming to you in a heartbeat.

It looks like I'll be home a couple of days before New Year's. This has been the longest few weeks of my life.

Guess I have to say, thoughts of that kiss have kept me going. Thank you.

Be there soon,

Welder Man

Dearest Denver,

Kissing isn't the only thing I'm thinking about.

I'll be in town to pick you up.

Love,

Natalie

Holy smokes, Natalie. You sure as shooting know how to make a man wish he could fly.

Denver

Denver's leg shook up and down. It was the only outward manifestation of his inward impatience.

He thought, anyway.

Jonathan didn't seem to notice.

He had gotten quiet, though.

Denver just hadn't been able to keep answering him.

He'd been counting down the minutes until he could see Natalie again.

It felt like he'd been gone years.

Despite the eighty hour workweeks and the long, cold days tossing in the sea, he'd found time to send four or five emails each day. Sometimes they weren't long, but all were heartfelt.

One each day to the kids – they were his, after all. He hoped they could eventually be a family.

The rest to Natalie.

It was hard for him to say all the things he felt. There just weren't words. He'd never thought of himself as someone who couldn't write, but he really couldn't write what was in his heart for his wife.

He also totally believed the saying, "Absence makes the heart grow fonder." That was absolutely true in his case.

He'd not wanted to leave, but being away had solidified his decision – he was hanging up his welding rod and wet suit and settling down on the farm.

Funny how a good woman made a decision like that easy.

He just hoped he could be the man she needed. Because of his job and the way he'd spent his life up to this point, he didn't have much experience in giving a woman what she needed. Let alone what she wanted, because he wanted to give her that, too.

He supposed he was well and truly smitten.

The thought made him smile.

He was still smiling ten minutes later when Jonathan finally pulled into the steak house parking lot where he'd picked Denver up what felt like an eternity ago.

"Thanks for the ride. Come visit sometime."

"Think I'll let you have a honeymoon first," Jonathan said with a smirk.

Denver barely heard him. He'd grabbed his bag from the back and slammed the door with a wave.

Natalie had gotten out of her SUV and stood at the back corner, waiting.

Jonathan drove away.

Denver flexed his jaw. Man, just looking at her made all the crazy pieces of his heart blend together in sweet harmony.

It also made his throat tight and his hands sweat.

He dropped his big duffle, and everything else he held.

Her brilliant blue eyes widened.

His feet started forward.

After all the weeks of waiting, he wasn't sure if he was ready, but when her lips turned up, that doubt soon vanished.

He caught her up in his arms and twirled her around. "This seems familiar," he murmured.

"Without the rain," she said back.

"What rain?" he asked with a grin which she returned. He'd barely noticed it and it never figured into his memories. Only her kiss.

"I want to kiss you," he said softly. "But I had a hard time stopping once I started the last time. I want to say hi to the kids, too." He glanced over at the tinted window.

Natalie's lip pulled in between her teeth. It caught his eye. His heart thumped harder and his hands tightened on her back.

"I...the kids are staying with Miss Penny tonight."

His lungs seized and his heart stopped. He wanted to be a family. Wanted to jump right in to being a dad and putting all the plans he had for the farm into motion.

But he also wanted to start being a husband.

He didn't want to make assumptions.

"She asked for them?" he said hesitantly.

"No." Natalie lifted her chin, her curly hair blowing with the wind. "I asked her to."

"Why?" he asked, softly, hoping he knew.

"I thought…" Natalie's eyes seemed to want to focus on his forehead. She met his gaze. "I thought we might want to finish that kiss."

"We're kissing tonight?" he asked, his palms burning. "You'd said you were thinking of other things?"

"I hoped you were too."

"I was. I definitely was. But that's not all I was thinking about."

"Oh?"

"No. I have ideas for the farm and for the house and the Christmas trees and the fruit trees and replanting and building and everything I want to do involves you and our children. I want this to be a family farm in the truest sense of the word."

Natalie's eyes closed. Her throat worked. A tear slipped out from one eye and trickled down her cheek.

He hoped it was a good tear. He couldn't bring himself to ask.

Finally, her eyes opened. "All my dreams just came true." The tear tracked a little farther and he brushed it with his thumb. "All except one."

His heart had leaped in his chest and swung in big circles around his rib. But at those words his brows furrowed. "Which one?"

"I still want to finish that kiss."

"Let's go home. Maybe once we're there, we can figure out where we left off."

Epilogue

rew Pittman slammed the door to his pickup shut and limped onto the sidewalk of Mistletoe, Arkansas.

Some days were worse than others.

Today was a bad one.

Cold weather didn't help. From what his friend, Denver, had told him, Arkansas wasn't usually this chilly. Didn't matter. He was going to live with the pain for the rest of his life.

He hated that he was barely thirty-one and walked like an old man.

He figured it made his chances of finding a wife less than they'd been before he'd gotten hurt.

Not that they'd been that great pre-accident.

Oh, before Denver had walked him down the church aisle, he'd been with plenty of women. Done plenty of things he wasn't real proud of, too – all after he'd loosened up with a beer. Or six.

It pretty much took a six pack, or a few shots of the hard stuff to loosen him up.

After that, he was smooth.

He'd given it all up, though.

Didn't really regret the lack.

Did miss the loss of inhibitions. Some of them anyway. Enough that he could talk to a girl at least.

It hadn't mattered when he could do his job. But now that he was crippled...

The bell above the door jingled as he walked into the coffee shop.

"Crew! Good to see you, man!" Denver, his big, calm, level-headed friend, stood as a straw paper flew by his head.

He raised a brow at a tow-headed boy who was lowering a straw from his mouth.

"You missed," he said with a grin.

"Won't next time," the kid said, a smirk in his voice.

"Go pick your paper up," Denver commanded, but his tone was underlaid with affection.

Then his whole face softened as his gaze swept the table and landed on the curly-haired woman sitting among four other little kids. Her brows raised and her lips turned up.

She shared a look so tender and sweet with Denver that it made Crew's chest ache. Denver was the kind of upright man who deserved to have a woman looking at him like that.

Crew had just made his mind up that he didn't really need a coffee and was getting ready to go see his new hundred acre farm on his own, when Denver winked at his wife, then turned to him.

"Glad you could make it, Buddy." He walked forward with his hand out.

"Good to be here."

"You're gonna love it here. Best farming ground in the country and the people are down-to-earth and hardworking. Best kind."

Crew jerked his head. He wasn't going to be doing much work with this crippled up body of his. Not the kind of work he was used to, anyway.

"I wanted to introduce you to my wife, Natalie." Denver's face took on that look again. The besotted look of a man in love. Crew would have made fun of him if he hadn't wanted to wear that look so badly himself.

"Good to meet you Natalie," Crew said, hating that he sounded stiff and slightly formal. He needed alcohol to relax around a woman. Since he didn't drink anymore, stiff and formal was all he did.

Natalie stood gracefully, a friendly smile on her face. "I'm so honored to meet you. Denver has told me so many stories of the things you guys have done – on ship and off."

Crew raised a brow at his friend. Their escapades had been harmless. And legal. At least half the time.

Denver introduced him to his children and Crew shook each little proffered hand. He'd never really thought of kids of his own. His childhood hadn't been the greatest, and he hadn't thought he'd be a very good dad. But Denver seemed to be a natural.

Maybe he could do it too. Same roadblock. Had to talk to a woman in order to have kids with her.

Before that, he'd probably have to explain his rather colorful past that included some things even Denver didn't know.

Alcohol wasn't enough of a numbing agent for some things. When that failed, there were drugs that could get him to where he needed to be.

All of that was behind him, though. Mistletoe was a fresh start. He just hoped he didn't screw this up.

Join Jessie's list and be the first to know about new releases and sales on her books!

Read Dreaming of Her Secret Santa's Kiss, the next book in the Cowboy Mountain Christmas series where Crew and Burgundy have secrets that could threaten everything when they come out. Keep reading for a sneak peek now.

Sneak Peek of Dreaming of Her Secret Santa's Kiss

Note from Jessie:

Sorry, I know it says "Chapter 1" here, but I wanted to make sure everyone saw this, and sometimes Amazon opens your kindle directly to Chapter 1, skipping everything before it.

Some of my ARC readers suggested a Trigger Warning for this book.

I thought that was a good idea, but, since I'm a story teller, I thought I'd tell you a story to let you know what might be in this book that could stir up some painful memories and feelings. I don't want you to read this book if it's going to hurt you or make you sad.

Back when I was a young mother I saw an interview on late night TV. I don't usually watch TV, but I'm guessing I was up with one of my babies. Maybe they were sick.

Anyway, some late-night TV host was interviewing a porn star.

I got married young and was a very young mother. That girl on TV was probably exactly my age.

She described some of the things she did, despicable things. Things I had never heard of or imagined. I think she shocked the shock jock as she removed her clothes and offered to do those despicable things to him.

I should have turned the TV off.

But my heart was broken.

Beyond her fake smile and false bravado and her seeming unconcern for any type of decency or modesty lay a soul that my God loved and died for.

To me, her pain was real. I could feel it just as sure as if I were sitting beside her and she were crying on my shoulder. For me, every word that came out of her mouth was a plea for love and acceptance – the kind that only God can give – and she was trying to fill that soul-deep need by any and all depravities known to man.

We were poor. We never had much. But I had been blessed beyond measure.

I knew, as I sat there, my heart hurting, that I could have had a different family, different parents, different school, made different choices, that, but for the grace of God, that girl could have been me.

I don't remember her name, don't know what happened to her. But she made a life-time impression on me, and I wanted to dedicate this book to her. Because she changed my life.

~Jessie Gussman, October 16, 2020

Burgundy Gannon rapped sharply on the dilapidated old farmhouse door, drawing a deep breath and trying to pretend this wasn't her last resort.

She was also trying to pretend her ankle didn't hurt.

She hadn't noticed the weak board on the porch steps a couple seconds ago. When she stepped on it and it gave way, she was unprepared. She didn't think she'd actually sprained her ankle, but it was definitely throbbing.

If she got the job, it would be worth it.

Of course, as run-down as the whole farm looked, maybe she should insist on prepayment.

Was having a job that she ended up not getting paid for better than not having a job at all?

The door opened before she could figure out the answer to that question. She thought it might be a no.

A wizened old lady appeared as the door cracked wider. Wild white hair stuck out in all directions from her head, and she wore bright green pants with an orange flowered shirt and a pink vest.

Black high-top Converse sneakers completed the outfit.

Even in LA, Burgundy's most recent address, this lady would be considered eccentric.

In Mistletoe, Arkansas? She was probably right up there with UFO sightings.

Her eyes looked shrewd, and they were narrowed as they looked Burgundy up and down.

If this lady, Mrs. Scholz, was an inch over four feet, it wasn't by much.

It didn't really matter how tall she was. Her eyes more than made up for any lack in height. It felt like she could see into Burgundy's heart and past and knew exactly what she was trying to hide.

The guilt that never quite completely left her slithered in her stomach, burning.

It always made her want to crumple in on herself.

She straightened her shoulders instead. The sins of her past were covered.

She knew it. Had knowledge. Sometimes, though, it was hard to remember and harder to believe. And even harder to act like it.

"State your business, or get gone."

The words were spit out, and they didn't really have an undertone of kindness in them.

Burgundy blinked, a little taken aback. But she didn't allow her shoulders to drop, nor did she step back.

She'd been in tougher places than this.

Of course, she'd taken worst jobs than this too.

That's why she needed this one so badly. There was always the temptation, no matter how far she was away from her past, to go back to it. If she needed it.

She knew there was something she could do to support herself.

Even if it was reprehensible.

She wanted to think she would die first.

But she knew she wouldn't. She was a survivor, not a martyr.

"Pastor Race sent me. He said you needed a caretaker."

There. Her voice was level, calm. With just the right amount of caring in it. Maybe Hollywood had passed her up, but she was still a good actress.

The woman's eyes narrowed, and her lips pursed, although the wrinkles in her face didn't straighten out. She looked Burgundy up and down, then up and down again.

Once more, Burgundy had that feeling like she'd been found wanting or that she'd been found out.

No one in this town knows what you are. Relax. They won't find out, unless you tell them.

Unless someone watches...

Not in this town. Not in middle America. That's for the big cities.

It wasn't true. She knew it wasn't true. She also knew it was shocking the people who might know her.

But in her movies, she had been a brunette.

For six months, she'd been a redhead.

That's why her hair was now platinum blonde.

She'd also straightened her natural curls out.

The glasses were part of her disguise as well.

"Well? What do you have to say for yourself? Are you just gonna stand there staring at me?"

"Race Steiner sent me. He said you were in need of a caretaker. That's what I am. A caretaker."

She was kind of proud of her acting skills.

She wasn't anything close to a caretaker.

Some of her coworkers would laugh at that.

All of them really. Because technically, maybe she *was* taking care of people. Men. In the loosest sense of the words.

She shoved the lewd jokes aside.

That was something else. She'd had to get used to a whole new way of thinking. Just little things would bring the words and the images and the jokes and the things she used to laugh about and the things that used to make her angry to the surface.

"You don't look like a caretaker," the woman spat out. Again, it didn't sound like there was any kindness in her voice. "You look like a sultry tramp who's out to steal my husband."

Maybe a shadow passed over the woman's eyes at the word husband. Burgundy couldn't be sure.

"'Course the man's been dead nigh on five years now. Which is why I need a caretaker."

If her voice was a little bit less rough, less sharp, it was hard to tell. Still, whether it was the shadow, or whether it was the idea of being married for such a long time, and thinking of her loss, her words made Burgundy feel bad.

"I'm sorry to hear that," she said again.

"Don't be. It's over and done with. He's currently the better off of the two of us."

Burgundy looked the woman up and down, trying to figure out what she meant by that.

Maybe if she got the job, the information would come out.

She hadn't exactly put her best foot forward.

But, in her defense, her best foot had a turned ankle that was throbbing right now.

She took a breath and held her hand out with the best smile that she could muster. She was really good at smiling when she didn't feel like it.

"I'm Burgundy, and I'm pleased to meet you, Mrs....?" She figured the woman was Mrs. if her husband had died years ago.

The woman looked at her hand with suspicion, like she suspected Burgundy was holding it out as some kind of trick.

Her jaw worked before she finally stuck her old gnarled hand into Burgundy's. Her fingers were crooked, but her grip was surprisingly firm.

Burgundy didn't flinch, but she might have if it hadn't been a little old lady squeezing her fingers.

Thankfully, she wasn't wearing any of the rings that she might have been if she were back in her old life.

It'd been a full year.

In some ways, it felt like forever, and in some ways, it wasn't nearly long enough.

"You can call me Mrs. Scholz. That's what everyone else does."

The lady seemed to speak reluctantly, like she wasn't wanting to give up any personal information, or maybe she just didn't want to like Burgundy. Maybe it was a mixture of the two.

"It's such a pleasure to meet you, Mrs. Scholz. Pastor Race has highly recommended me. Here's the letter he wrote that he said I could deliver to you, to help you make up your mind."

Her fingers trembled ever so slightly as she pulled the note out of her purse and handed it to Mrs. Scholz.

Mrs. Scholz looked suspiciously at the paper and Burgundy's hand.

Everyone in Mistletoe had been super friendly to her. She'd even made a few dollars waitressing at the small coffee shop when the regular waitress spent two days visiting her mother.

She'd made a little more money selling Christmas trees for a couple of weeks before Christmas.

Both of those jobs had expiration dates though, and if she

wanted to stay in a small town, which she did, she needed to find something that she could do that would pay enough for her to stay.

Maybe one time, her tastes ran to fancy. Not anymore.

Mrs. Scholz did not invite her in but stood in the doorway as she opened the letter and read down through it.

Burgundy had quit smoking, but she supposed the craving for a cigarette would never completely go away.

This was one of those times.

Not that she necessarily wanted the nicotine, she just wanted to have something to do with her hands.

She had been one of the lucky few who could do drugs without getting addicted to them. At least she never had. She supposed everyone had their tipping point.

It was only by the grace of God that she hadn't reached hers.

In her old life, it wasn't hard to see what drugs did to a person.

Mrs. Scholz seemed to be done reading the paper, but her head was still down, like she was thinking.

Behind her, there was a shout and a couple of dogs barking and what sounded like someone pounding.

Burgundy didn't turn to look. It was a farm, or something like that, and she supposed there were animals on it and people working. Made sense.

She also supposed that the animals wouldn't come up on the porch and try to get in the house, so she felt like she was safe standing there with her back toward everything.

"Well, might be against my better judgment, but I do have a tendency to trust what Pastor Race says." The woman's eyes were shrewd as she looked at Burgundy. "I'm gonna have to start you at half my regular rate, since you have no experience."

"You have a regular rate?" Burgundy had been under the impression that she was the first housekeeper that Mrs. Scholz had hired.

"I do." Mrs. Scholz named minimum wage.

Burgundy bit her tongue. Hard. The metallic taste of blood seeped into her mouth. Not unfamiliar.

She wasn't quite sure what Mrs. Scholz had suggested was legal.

Not that she was a stickler for being legal.

At least, she had never been before.

She'd changed. For the most part.

It was hard not to think of the money that she'd made in her previous profession.

Half of minimum wage wouldn't even pay for one minute.

But the work was wrong. And she was ashamed of it. And no matter how much she made, she wouldn't go back.

God, will I always be tempted?

She wasn't tempted because she loved her work; she could almost get to the point where she separated it as a job in her head. She didn't have to like what she was doing in order to do it.

She just did her best at her job.

Ugh. She was lying to herself, and she knew it. By the very virtue that it was her with her voice, her body, or both, it didn't matter. It was a job, yes, but it was a job she could have refused.

But she didn't.

"I suppose you can come in if you're accepting. You're not very talkative."

Too many memories.

"I'm sorry. I'll accept. How long is the probationary rate?"

"Two weeks," Mrs. Scholz said shortly. "If you're satisfactory, I'll raise it to minimum wage." She stepped back, and Burgundy stepped in. "We'll discuss it six months from then if we're both satisfied and talk about where we're going from there."

Mrs. Scholz might be a little lady, and kind of bent over, with gnarled fingers, but her mind was sharp as a tack anyway.

She walked in the house, which was cluttered to say the least.

Race hadn't given her all the details. He'd been called out to try to counsel a couple involved in the middle of a fight that involved breaking dishes and crying little children.

He'd given Burgundy the barest of details, handed her the letter, and told her he had to go.

"That sounds fine, Mrs. Scholz." Part of the job was that she would have a room in which to stay and food to eat.

She really didn't have ambition beyond that. Hiding out and putting her past behind her.

It would just take time.

She closed the rickety door behind her with a sigh. Knickknacks covered every surface. Burgundy tried hard to figure out a theme, but it seemed to be geese mixed with mushrooms mixed with pink flamingos maybe?

The rug she stood on sported a purple dinosaur.

Maybe the cohesive theme was that there was no cohesive theme.

Mrs. Scholz walked through a door on the right. "Obviously, this is the kitchen. I can cook. But the social worker that was in here said I should have supervision, which I completely disagree with, but in order to stay..." Her voice trailed off, and there was that shadow again.

Burgundy tried to set her past aside. Mrs. Scholz obviously had some pain in her past as well.

"You might as well know it now. I sold the farm. But," her eyes got crafty, "I made the sucker who bought it promise that I could stay here until I died. He insisted that I had to have a caretaker. So that's why you're here. He's afraid I'll burn the house down by leaving the oven on." The old lady shifted. "Maybe he's right. I have forgotten a time or two. But doesn't everyone?"

Burgundy nodded. "Actually, I have. I'm horrible at remembering to turn it off. I get involved in other things, and I've left it on all night before."

"Exactly! That's exactly what I told him. So normal."

Burgundy grinned and nodded.

Mrs. Scholz didn't exactly grin at her, but she felt like maybe they had a tenuous bond trying to form between them, united against whoever it was that had bought her house.

"So, there's someone else living here too?"

Those crafty old eyes shifted back, and the old lady nodded. "I can't believe Pastor Race didn't tell you that."

"He was kinda busy."

Which was fine. It didn't matter whether there was someone else living here or not. Although, she couldn't help the little tremolo of fear that gripped her heart every time she thought of meeting someone new.

Would they recognize her? Would they know who she was?

So far, she hadn't gotten the impression that anyone in Mistletoe knew. She'd really like to keep it that way.

Although, she kinda had a feeling that one's past had a tendency to catch up with one, and she doubted she was the exception to that rule. She hadn't been the exception to any others.

"Did you bring your stuff with you?" Mrs. Scholz tilted her head around as though looking for a bag would make one materialize near Burgundy.

"I have a couple of suitcases and a duffel out in my car."

It was everything she had in the world. When she'd hit rock bottom, she didn't have much left worth salvaging.

Most of the clothes she had were clothes that she'd gotten after she'd been rescued.

"Might as well go out and get them, bring them in here. We'll take them upstairs and show you to your room." Mrs. Scholz crossed her arms over her chest and stood back. Something about the discordance of her outfit made her blend right into the discordance of the house décor.

Funny how things seemed to suit each other.

Burgundy just hoped she found something that suited her.

As she walked out to her car, she saw a couple cows over by the barnyard, but no people.

Her heart wouldn't let her rest until she met the new owner of the farm and found out, by looking at his face, whether or not he knew her.

Her suitcase bounced along behind her as she limped back to the house. Her ankle wasn't twisted and would probably be fine, if a little stiff in the morning.

She walked up the porch steps a little more carefully this time.

She followed Mrs. Scholz upstairs, past piles of family pictures on the walls and shelves of knickknacks. She was careful not to bump them, even though she was a little off balance with her suitcases. That was not the kind of inauspicious beginning she wanted.

They took a right and went down to the far room. Mrs. Scholz opened the door.

"This is yours. It don't have too much stuff in it. It took me two weeks to clean this one out. Hope you're happy with it."

The bedroom was at the back of the house, with great big windows that stretched almost from the floor to the ceiling, giving her a gorgeous view of the backyard and what she assumed were pasture fields. She was more than happy.

The beauty outside more than beat the dingy window view of her apartment in LA. Even with the amount of money she made, she'd never had a great place to live.

Drugs were expensive.

"This is perfect. Thank you."

"Got some warm 'ems up we can have for supper. You can start cooking tomorrow." Mrs. Scholz started to back out the door. "We eat at six, whether that man is here or not."

Burgundy's eyebrows went up at that, but she didn't make a comment.

That man.

The way Mrs. Scholz spat that out made it sound like she didn't care for the guy.

"I'll be down early to help set the table."

She could earn her keep. But she did appreciate the chance to settle in.

As soon as the door closed, she went to her handbag and pulled out a ratty-looking gray stuffed elephant.

"Oh, Rosemary. Here we are. Another new spot. We probably can't put our roots down here, either. But maybe we can try putting out a few tentacles. We have to get the stuffy Mrs. Scholz to love us or at least like us a little."

She stroked down the soft gray fur and then squeezed the animal to her chest.

Rosemary had gone with her from move to move to move, although she hadn't gotten her until after the worst moment of her life.

She'd not been there when the first boy was in her bedroom at thirteen.

She'd not been there when she'd been voted "most popular" in her high school freshman class.

She'd not gone on overnight cheerleading trips.

And she'd not gone along on the senior class trip, when she shared a room—and a bed—with Todd and Brian.

"Why weren't you there to tell me that was wrong?" she asked Rosemary, holding the elephant away and looking into the one eye that was still attached. Most of the gray fur had been rubbed off. She looked lumpy and was probably filthy.

Burgundy would never give her up.

Rosemary didn't have to answer anyway. Burgundy might not have had moral teaching, and everybody had been telling her from the time she was little that it was okay as long as she used protection. Which she had.

But her heart had told her it was wrong.

Her conscience, her soul, her spirit. It never felt right. It might have been fun, and she'd always made sure she enjoyed herself.

But it never felt right.

Man, she wished she could go back and do it all over again. So much she'd do different

"We're starting over, Rosemary." She kissed the elephant and set her on the bed. Now, the room felt like hers.

Sign up for Jessie's newsletter! Get a free book, access to exclusive bonus content, get fun and funny updates on her life on the farm and more!

Read More Jessie!

Tap here to see all of Jessie's books!

A Gift from Jessie

View this code through your smart phone camera to be taken to a page where you can download a FREE ebook when you sign up to get updates from Jessie Gussman! Find out why people say, "Jessie's is the only newsletter I open and read" and "You make my day brighter. Love, love, love reading your newsletters. I don't know where you find time to write books. You are so busy living life. A true blessing." and "I know from now on that I can't be drinking my morning coffee while reading your newsletter – I laughed so hard I sprayed it out all over the table!"

Claim your free book from Jessie!

Escape to more faith-filled romance series by Jessie Gussman!

The Complete Sweet Water, North Dakota Reading Order:

Series One: Sweet Water Ranch Western Cowboy Romance (11 book series)

Series Two: Coming Home to North Dakota (12 book series)

Series Three: Flyboys of Sweet Briar Ranch in North Dakota (13 book series)

Series Four: Sweet View Ranch Western Cowboy Romance (10 book series)

Spinoffs and More! Additional Series You'll Love:

Jessie's First Series: Sweet Haven Farm (4 book series)

Small-Town Romance: The Baxter Boys (5 book series)

Bad-Boy Sweet Romance: Richmond Rebels Sweet Romance (3 book series)

Sweet Water Spinoff: Cowboy Crossing (9 book series)

Small Town Romantic Comedy: Good Grief, Idaho (5 book series)

True Stories from Jessie's Farm: Stories from Jessie Gussman's Newsletter (3 book series)

Reader-Favorite! Sweet Beach Romance: Blueberry Beach (8 book series)

Blueberry Beach Spinoff: Strawberry Sands (10 book series)

From Strawberry Sands to: Raspberry Ridge (12 book series)

Swoonfully Jolly Holiday Stories:

Holiday Romance: Cowboy Mountain Christmas (6 book series)

Cowboy Mountain Christmas Spinoff: A Heartland Cowboy Christmas (9 book series)

New and Much Loved: Mistletoe Meadows (4 books and counting!)

Laughing Through the Snow: Christmas Tree, PA Sweet Romcoms (6 short reads)